Struggle and Survival, A Boneyard Saga, Short Story Anthology

Mona Lisa on the Moon Series

George and Linda B

ISBN: 979-8-9864589-8-4
eISBN: 979-8-9864589-9-1

Preface

The following short stories are stand-alone tales but are part of a larger saga about living in and around the Yellowstone National Park. One hundred thousand years ago, the characters struggled against the top predators of the late Pleistocene. The skills needed to survive such a hostile environment were considerable. Interestingly, the extreme conditions found in the ancient past are very similar to those found today. Eva, the main character grew from a young, deformed child into a powerful woman. Throughout, she defied all odds to become the unchallenged leader of her people and the mother of future generations that populate the known galaxies.

The people group covered in this series lived most of the time in the Boneyard. The Clan had a territory that covered several hundred square miles. At the center of this area, was a group of thermals that belched heat, steam, and sulfuric gases all year round. This area attracted animals of all types, especially during the bitterly cold winter months and many of the sojourners were killed or died there, leaving their bones as a temporary reminder of their fate. The area was thus known by the Clan as The Boneyard. This place was the hunting ground of last resort because it held a fearful, mystical, and magnetic quality that both attracted and repelled humans and most likely other animals as well. The dominant species, other than humans were the Terror Birds. They were the Apex Predators of the Megafauna of the late Pleistocene. They were flightless, standing over eight feet tall and weighed in at a of minimum of 330 pounds. It was estimated they could run more than forty miles an hour for short bursts.

Connected to these short stories is a book known as the "Mona Lisa on the Moon Collection." The first book published in the series is titled "Volume 1, Mona Lisa on the Moon, Thirty-Two Thousand Years in the Making."

SCIENCE FICTION

Thirty-two thousand years ago, a gifted child is born into a world most would consider paradise. There has not been a war or hunger for some eight thousand years. The ozone layer is four times thicker than it will be later. Genetic abnormalities are nearly nonexistent and there are no diseases. As she matures, Mona Ann Lisa—just one of a highly advanced civilization on Earth—prepares to fulfill her destiny.

Unbeknownst to Mona, a change in the political and military leadership has been ongoing for decades. Now something new is afoot. After she eventually becomes the youngest captain of the planet's fleet of spaceships, her career blossoms as she faces challenges and threats to her civilization. Mona is the best chance the species has to survive. While she accepts her many working titles, Mona knows that Levie, her sentient artificial intelligence entity, is the true brains of the operations. As a chain of events unfolds, Mona, Levie, and others must jump into action as the health and well-being of all sentient life precariously hangs in the balance.

In this science fiction novel set thirty-two thousand years ago, a child prodigy transforms into the captain of a fleet of spaceships and embarks on a journey to save humanity.

"I recently enjoyed a science fiction themed story about ancient space explorers, originally from our own Planet Earth, and ultimately responsible for the health and well being of all sentient life in the known universe. The story, although supported by complex and advanced scientific fact as well as fantasy, has been told in a way that appeals to any age group. I, as well as many other readers, have been absolutely enthralled with this story of fantasy, that always made us convinced these adventures, and characters, were as real as anyone we may have met in our lifetimes. This kind of composing genius needs to be shared with the reading public. The soon to be popular author is George Berberich."

—*Karen Hatcher*

U.S. $XX.XX

VOLUME 1,
MONA LISA ON THE MOON,
Thirty-Two Thousand Years in the Making

GEORGE B.

Short Story
Table of Contents

The Boneyard

Short Story 1
Short Story by George and Linda B

Eva and Credo were alone at the outskirts of the Boneyard to survey the Clan's chances of locating food. Though it was early morning, she did not expect to encounter a Terror Bird. While an attack was possible, Eva's intuition told her they were temporarily safe. Credo had alerted on a dragonfly and was preoccupied by its erratic flight. She quickly gave Credo hand signals to ignore the large insect and to instead survey the surrounding perimeter.

Credo was always at Eva's side unless she ordered otherwise. He bonded with her at his birth five cycles ago. Eva was a leader of her people and was worthy of his attention and loyalty. Others of his kind were not as lucky. Saber cats were intensely hunted by Eva's tribe, the two species competed for the same food resources. One of Credo's eyes was damaged at birth, and he would not have survived without this symbiotic partnership with his human benefactor. Eva was flawed also. Her left leg was deformed and her ability to hunt was thus limited. However, her keen sight, hearing and intuition assisted by Credo's legs and enormous strength made them the best providers of the entire Clan. The two were inseparable and were relied upon to find game when others failed.

Eva's value was significant because of her second sense when it came to reading hunting signs. She could also anticipate changes in weather conditions. She felt impending danger before others and was the early warning system for all that fell under her care. The Clan had a territory that covered several hundred square miles. At the center of this area, was a group of thermals that belched heat, steam and sulfuric gases all year round. This area attracted animals of all types, especially during the bitterly cold winter months and many of the sojourners were killed or died there, leaving their bones as a temporary reminder of their fate. The area was thus known by the Clan as The Boneyard. This place was the hunting ground of last resort because it held a fearful, mystical, and magnetic quality that both attracted and repelled humans and most likely other animals as well. The dominant species, other than humans were the Apex Predators of the Megafauna of the late Pleistocene. However, the most feared and formidable was the Terror Bird, it was flightless, was over eight feet tall and weighed approximately 330 pounds. Their heads were large, with huge, axe-like beaks. Being enormously quick and vicious, they ran at speeds exceeding forty miles an hour in short spurts. These birds could track, attack and kill prey much larger than themselves. They worked in groups of two or more and were intelligent, and fearless. This species always came to the Boneyard during specific seasons and Eva was very aware of their customary behavior.

However, this year was particularly bad for hunting and the Clan was pushed to take more chances than they have normally. Eva and Credo were critical to the tribe's survival. She knew she could not make a mistake. An error on her part could result in her death and the possible demise of the entire Clan.

In desperation Eva headed for the Boneyard. Though the risks were great the Boneyard represented the only true guarantee for food. Eva knew the Terror Birds would most likely be there as well. The Clan's weapons were spears and slings along with their coordination, unity of purpose and their capacity to adapt to changing and dangerous events. While alert and in a hunting party, her people could adequately defend themselves. However, as individuals or in small groups, humans were too slow and vulnerable, unable to defend against two or more Terror Birds if the attack was in unison. During resting periods and at night the danger was at its peak. These birds loved to hunt in the early evening and early morning hours. Eva maintained watchmen all day long and deep into the night to alert for any danger. Other than these terrible flightless birds, the Dire Wolves who weighed an average of 150 pounds were a concern because they were also pack hunters. Fortunately, since the Clan was in bird territory the wolves were not going to be present. The wolves feared the birds more than the humans.

Eva was concerned and more frustrated than normal because her people had been decimated through disease and starvation. The older members and the very young could travel no more and without enough food the entire Clan's endurance was at its end. Being now half their normal numbers, the Clan could not both man multiple hunting parties and adequately protect the elderly and children. Eva had to find a solution and was desperate to do so. At this point the Boneyard would be the best answer to the Clan's need for a food source. Eva decided to put every able body out to gather food and hunt, praying the worst would not happen. While pondering the serious issues in front of her, Eva remembered a dream she had not long ago. The stones from a mountain fell on her and Credo. She expected to die, instead they survived without a scratch. Could this dream have been pointing her to the survival or inevitable destruction of her Clan? This was a puzzle she had to solve soon.

Eva was thinking, The Boneyard might just be their last stand, but was jolted back to the reality, when she saw Credo returning from his survey of the thermals. He was acting differently shown by his speed and directness of approach. Eva sensed his excitement. This meant food or danger and maybe both. In anticipation, she took out her sling and place a large stone in it. As he approached, he made a set of quick clicking sounds "kee, kik, kee, kik" She knew to follow him immediately.

As they rounded a small thermal pool of green and orange algae, the billowing steam was blown away by a stiff breeze to reveal a set of five crude nests on the ground. The nests were full of several very large eggs. Eva knew immediately these were Terror Bird eggs. Because of her desperation she didn't hesitate, she grabbed her carrying pouch and put as many eggs in it as she could. She then fashioned a drag from long leg bones and placed several more eggs on it to take them back to the camp. She knew the Birds would follow her trail as soon as they discovered the missing treasure, but this was survival. She was ready to accept the consequences of her actions. At this very moment, Eva knew the Terror Birds could be attacking her vulnerable and unprotected clansmen. This may well be a war of mutually assured destruction.

With her deformed leg her return with the added weight of the eggs was excruciating. She was weak for lack of food and knew she had little time to escape. Credo kept a constant watch for the birds. He moved around her, first in a wide circle and then kept getting closer and closer to her as they got further from the Boneyard.

As she returned to the camp, the old and young greeted her with warm hugs and talk. They wanted to hear the whole story, but she was too busy trying to share the eggs with the Clan. She soon collapsed from fatigue, and they placed furs over her. Credo lay beside her. She slept for several hours and had the nightmare again about the landslide. When she awoke, she and Credo were given all the Terror Bird egg stew they could eat. The others who were out hunting returned without anything but shared in the eggs to their fill. Eva knew this was the calm before the storm. She ordered fires be started and maintained around the perimeter and she and Credo left the encampment.

Eva didn't know just what she was looking for, but she knew she would recognize it when she saw it. The place the Clan was now living was too vulnerable to stay much longer. After a half-hour journey, she began to wonder if she was going crazy. What was she looking for?

She spotted a pile of large rocks and boulders. The pile looked like the results of a recent landslide. A large cave would have been better but there were none in this area and even if there were, her people would have to fight a family of cave bears for it. Never a good idea.

As she and Credo were climbing around the base of the pile, she heard the most frightening shrieks and screams she had ever heard. It was undeniable, the sounds were coming from the direction of the encampment. She immediately signaled Credo to run ahead. She followed as fast as she could. Upon arrival, one Terror Bird lay dead near the main fire pit and two clansmen were badly injured. It looked like one of the injured would soon die. Eva knew the war was now engaged.

Eva was told up to five Terror Birds had attacked the camp. They circled it and then rushed the adult defenders from two separate sides. While the two flanks were being attacked, a single bird came from a third direction toward the children who were surrounding the central fire pit. One of the elder men got off a perfect sling rock that hit the bird in one of its eyes. Two adults left the perimeter defense and attacked the injured bird with spears. The attacker was mortally wounded but had badly mauled the two adult defenders. After the bird was killed the rest retreated.

Eva was proud of her people but knew there would be future attacks. Unless her Clan left, the birds would continue the assault. The price was high but, in the end, they got some food and defended themselves. They would live to fight another day.

Eva slept that night but wrestled with her thoughts. The injured and the dying concerned her, but she would have sacrificed herself as they did for the same reasons. She was without mate or child because she was deformed. The ways of her people demanded that from her. She knew no other life. Her parents had long since succumbed to starvation. Credo was now her family. He was her child and companion. Her duty was to lead her people and help them survive and eventually thrive again. The weather had been harsh, and the rain had vanished for months now. There was hope the snows would come and next spring would return to normal, but she was afraid only the bitter cold would come instead. If they survived this winter, they might have to leave their hunting grounds to find other territory. This too might be a death sentence. They would most likely have to fight other Clans and other species to venture into their hunting grounds.

The hope was that with deep snow, hunting and tracking the scarce game would be made easier. The surviving bison would be encumbered by the snow and come into the range of the Clan's spears and slings. She knew she could not leave, she had to fight the Terror Birds for what little game existed until the snows came. Her people were as desperate as she knew the birds were, possibly only one species would triumph, and Eva intended it to be her Clan. At least the killed Terror Bird would feed the group for several days and might give them the strength to accomplish much more than just surviving a few more days.

When Eva woke in the early morning Credo was already sniffing around the main fire pit for breakfast. Some cooked bird sounded like a good start to his day. Eva went over to the fire and cut off some large chunks off the carcass and gave it to Credo who devoured it quickly ending the repast without anything but a loud burp and the licking of his lips and paws. He purred and rubbed his long powerful body against Eva to thank her for his meal.

Eva felt it was time to call a meeting to discuss what was next. All were present, young, old, and injured, a total of maybe fifty people. The badly wounded male was still alive and was showing signs of improvement. The herbal based antibiotic bandages, laced with sulfur had prevented infection from taking the warrior's life. The injuries were severe; however, the clansman presently was without infection and food was available, and if this continued survival was possible.

Eva could count on possibly fifteen strong adults that could do some heavy lifting. Her plan was simple but strenuous. She was going to move the Clan to the landslide and dig down and remove smaller rocks, silt, and dirt from between the larger boulders; making spaces where her people could fit within the rocks. The Clan had never tried anything like this. Their winter home had been moss, leaves, pelts and furs lining snow caves built into drifts of snow. In her mind, this excavation was not a permanent home but a safe room for the people left behind when the warriors went out to hunt and gather. This way the predators could not get to the young, wounded and elders. The openings for the clansmen would be sized to allow their entrance but not their predators. Theoretically, a few spears wielded by the elderly would protect the narrow entrances from even the strongest, largest and most enthusiastic attacker. Thus, Eva's landslide would now become the fortress for her people. Now the dream made sense!

She was in a race to move the Clan and start excavation before the Birds attacked again. Eva sent Credo to circle the formation as they moved, he would alarm them if the Birds were gathering for a new attack. She chided and pushed her fellow clansmen to move quickly. They built drags for the two injured warriors and kept the young and old in the center of their formation. No one went out to hunt or gather, they stayed within sight and touch of each other. Though Eva got to the rock pile in thirty minutes before, this group would take two hours to make the same journey.

Initially, things went smoothly but within an hour Credo gave a warning growl. The others did not understand but Eva knew immediately. She had one of the men climb a tree and act as look out. She sent out an advanced guard of two warriors to do the same thing. She then sent five ahead to secure the rock pile. While on the move the group was most vulnerable. Within a few minutes of Credo's warning. two Terror Birds appeared in front of the group. Two then appeared to their rear.

Suspecting the same tactics from the previous attack, Eva yelled, "Warriors align yourselves on both sides of our people. Expect the birds to strike from any direction. Now!" Within seconds, two birds surged from the underbrush towards the middle of the right flank of the group. In spite of their immediate response to Eva's orders, one bird got to their center and killed two children instantly. The other bird never made it to the defenders. He was hit with several sling rocks and run through by at least three spears. The bird that reached the core of the Clan sliced straight through and had disappeared into the underbrush. Eva ordered everyone to get down and to light torches. Hoping the fire would discourage a new assault.

After an hour there were no new attacks. Credo gave Eva an all clear growl and she ordered the Clan to pick up the dead children and butcher the lifeless bird. Within a few minutes the group was on its way to the rock pile. She grieved for the two lost children but understood the way of life. They had survived by eating the bird's eggs and these vicious birds had returned the favor. When and how this would end was now beyond her comprehension. They soon arrived at the landslide.

Eva gave the order to make camp. She placed lookouts on the top of the rocks and had the pile become the rear flank of the encampment. She sent several of the children with torches to look for gaps, cracks and clefts in the pile. Within a couple of hours, the group had settled down for the night. The pile was so irregular, she felt the birds could not easily negotiate it with any speed or ability to launch an attack.

She ordered all the brush and small trees removed in a wide arc around the camp and the rocks. The group worked continually for hours before they sat down to eat and mourn the death of the two children. Their custom was to leave the bodies of the dead in trees on small platforms. Because of their situation, they didn't want to leave the children's bodies for the Terror Birds, so Eva ordered them cremated. The Clan built a large fire pit on the outside of the encampment and burned their remains. The drought had made the availability of materials to build large funeral pyres very easy.

Eva did not sleep. She wondered all night if their enemies would return. She had lost two children and had two badly injured warriors. She had killed two of the enemy and destroyed most of their next generation of chicks. The eggs she took to feed her Clan were probably the last or only clutch before winter. To her knowledge, their small population, indicated they didn't reproduce frequently, and then few hatchlings even survive into adulthood. So, their actions might have already struck deeply at their survival numbers for future generations. So be it. It was now a war of extinction as far as she was concerned.

Eva decided the Clan would not move again before thaw. This was now their winter home and maybe to become their four seasons home. Until now she had never considered such a thing. However, the food was available here all year long. The only reason they didn't stay before was the Terror Birds. Necessity caused by drought had brought them here and the elimination of the Terror Birds might change their entire fortunes for generations to come.

Several days after the Clan settled into the new camp, Credo laid with his body next to his guardian and purred delightfully, she was deep in thought. Eva was planning an offensive. She mused: *now that the pile is properly prepared and fortified, it is a haven for the clansmen and the hunted become the hunters. I know where their nests are.* She wondered: *are they intelligent enough to move to a new location?* It was obvious to Eva the Birds had never feared discovery. The Thermals had been their safe place for eons. It provided warmth, camouflage, and even obliterated their scent because of the sulfur laced gasses. Eva thought; *Credo discovered it and we will exploit it again, If they are not able to adapt and nest elsewhere, next year will be their fall. Next year will be their end!* .

The Snows Return to the Boneyard

Short Story 2

Short Story by George and Linda B

Preface

As a diminutive child living in the late Pleistocene, Eva had defied all norms. She was born with a deformed left leg, leaving her crippled. Her constant companion Credo, was a half blind apex predator. Neither had been expected to survive to adulthood. However, they not only survived but ascended to the highest levels of responsibility, honor and leadership.

Eva remembered when she first saw Credo. He was a small kitten sized fur ball found by her father when the Clan discovered his dead mother in a cave near one of their camp sites. Two other offspring were found but were already dead. That was five cycles ago and Eva pleaded with her parents to allow her to keep the young animal. Since food was then abundant, her parents and the Clan leadership relented because they expected Credo would get lost, die or would have an unexpected lethal accident before he could reach maturity.

Before reaching adulthood, Eva became the uncontested leader of her Clan and Credo, an enormous saber cat, became the deadliest and most effective hunter. By tribal custom, Eva could not marry and therefore would not have offspring who could carry her deformity into future generations. She, therefore, dedicated all her energies to lead and provide for the Clan, leaving behind any hope or thought of her own family or children. She rose to leadership because of her intuition and intelligence. She could anticipate danger and read subtle hunting signs no other clansman could. Her understanding of weather changes was phenomenal. The unlikely two provided early warning to danger and became the best providers of all the warriors actively hunting for the group.

Additionally, Eva was an excellent marksman and deadly with her sling, which she always carried. Unlike the other warriors, she carried a bone hatchet instead of a long spear because her size and handicap made carrying a spear ineffective. Credo, a massive and powerful saber cat, was her equalizer. He was her constant companion and family, as well as protector. He relied on her because he was blind in one eye. Separately they were vulnerable but together they were more than a match, able to defeat any existing single predator. They had their own language; Eva used hand signals and he used his deep grunt-like sounds to respond.

Historical Notes Postscript

Before the beginning of this story, the Terror Birds, being flightless and weighing an average of 330 pounds each were able to run up to forty miles an hour, protected at least five nests, with five or more eggs in each. Eva had robbed these nests to feed her starving Clan last summer, initiating a war of attrition between the species. Now well fed, she along with her Clan had come to finish the job, the objective was to force the extinction of a vicious competitor.

The Snows Return to the Boneyard
Short story by George and Linda B

The snows came and the Terror Bird attacks became ineffective. The birds raided the camp weekly for three months but lost one or more combatants with every assault. Eva's tribe used the failed incursions to supplement their hunting. The Clan had a steady diet of Terror Bird along with the bison that was now available because of the early snow. Her people were now better fed than at any time in her memory, which made the loss of half her people to starvation (including her own parents) all the more tragic. In addition, to the two badly wounded warriors had since recovered from the previous Terror Bird mauling and except for the death of two children to the birds, most other things were going very well. However, as the Clan Leader, Eva was in a quandary of what to do as summer approached.

Credo, Eva's massive Saber cat, was lying next to her and was almost asleep. She was scratching the furry ear nearest to her and pondering the future. The loud purr was hypnotic. Eva was almost in a twilight and suddenly had a violent vision. It was like a lightning bolt hitting the optic nerve. The jolt was almost painful. Her body jerked violently. Growling Credo, menacingly, alerted and jumped into a defensive stance. There was a pungent odor and temporary paralysis. This had never happened before.

Once Eva recovered from the shock, she tried to focus on the vision. It was difficult but once her heart slowed and her vision cleared, a few memories emerged. An attack was in progress. She could not identify who or what was attacking. Credo was lunging at something. Screams were loudly penetrating her ears and Eva felt more fear than she could remember. Then everything vanished except her fear. She was breathing deeply and sweating even though (just before sunrise) the temperature was below freezing.

It was now a few days after Eva's frightening vision. Eva decided to lead a hunting party to the Boneyard. At the end of last summer Credo had discovered the Terror Bird nesting area hidden between the thermals in the Boneyard. These thermals belched steam and sulfuric gases year-round, providing heat and camouflage from any predators like a small pack of determined humans. The Boneyard got its name from the Clan because the area attracted species of animals drawn by the heat during the bitter winter months. Many of the animals died there leaving a concentration of bones as a reminder they once lived.

The objective was now to return to the nesting area of the Terror Birds and disrupt, destroy and eliminate any eggs or chicks that were found. The party was made up of half of the best warriors in the Clan. Credo was in the lead and circled the outer perimeter of the thermals. Eva was apprehensive.

The danger of engaging a group of Terror Birds on their turf was nuts. Eva knew this venture was very, very risky. However, her highly tuned intuition told her the risk was worth taking. Up to this point the Clan had lost two members and two more badly wounded by the birds. Over the last four months of their war, the birds had lost at least fifteen with many more wounded. If the clansmen had not been highly trained hunters with sophisticated coordination they would have been easy prey to any animal three-times their weight and three times faster. No other apex predator, including a wolf pack, would have attempted what they were doing.

Credo suddenly appeared like magic from behind a cloud of white mist coming from a hot pool, colored by orange, green and blue algae. His vocalization told Eva he had relocated the nesting area. Eva's heart was in her throat. She swallowed deeply and followed Credo. The warriors formed a defensive circle behind her and remained there until she returned or summoned them.

As Eva approached Credo she felt his uneasiness. His muscles were rigid and teeth more visible than usual. They both were anticipating an attack. Never-the-less, Eva led forward. Within a few minutes, the two cleared the billowing steam clouds and saw the nesting area. There were only two crude nests both boasting two eggs. This nesting area was a far cry from last summer's discovery of at least five nests with five or more eggs each. Upon closer examination, the eggs in one nest were ruined. They had been cracked and were rotting. Was it possible the Terror Birds were doomed? Eva was both pleased and somehow saddened. Her most feared enemy may well cease to exist in the not to distant future.

Then it happened! To her utter surprise, a Terror Bird rushed from the white mist. She barely had time to react. The screams and shriek were ear shattering. The sound alone was disorienting. Her instinctive reaction was to jump for the ground. Her fear was so strong she could taste it. This was her vision. She knew it immediately. The bird was too close to have used the sling. She had a bone club but it was no match for the huge axe-like beak of the bird. She rolled at the last instant to avoid the head and claws of the enormous bird. Credo lunged onto the bird's back as he moved downward to maul Eva. The cat's claws and enormous teeth severed the spine of the attacker. Both fell forward almost crushing the tiny Eva. The bird's clawed legs thrashed in lethal spasm. Eva had just enough time to avoid being vivisected. Within a few moments it was over. Credo and Eva survived. The enormous bird now dead. Eva thought it was not her time to die, maybe later today but not just now! The rest of the hunting party arrived in time to see the last spasms in the Terror Bird's limbs. Eva directed the party to clean and butcher the bird, to collect the two good eggs and return to the camp. Credo was given a large portion of the bird as reward. He devoured it with gusto.

Was this the end to the war? Did they just wipe out the last of the enemy? Somehow Eva thought not. If these demons were as intelligent as she thought, they would not be that easy to eradicate. The party left with speed and caution. Their guard was up and remained so all the way back to their camp.

Within earshot of the encampment, Credo alerted. He looked at Eva and she signed him to run ahead. Within a few minutes Credo's warning was heard by all. They instinctively knew their clansmen were under attack. While she and the hunting party took the bait at the Boneyard, a major assault was being waged against their people. Before leaving that morning, Eva, had ordered the elderly, young and injured to secure themselves into the gaps in the rock pile behind their camp. Able warriors, who remained in camp to take on any threat, were instructed to retreat to the rocks if the enemy was overwhelming

When Eva and the hunting party arrived, the camp was in shambles. Some ten terror birds were running around attempting to kill or destroy anything human. Eva ordered everyone in her party to remain hidden. They skirted the camp's perimeter and climbed the rock pile from the rear most approach. Once all were at the top, Eva ordered her people to rain down a barrage of stones and spears upon the rampaging Birds. Within seconds, three birds lay dead and three more were significantly wounded. The four unhurt birds immediately retreated, and the wounded hobbled off.

To Eva's relief, they had not lost a single member of the tribe. A couple were slightly injured in the hurried retreat to the gaps in the rocks. They had actually badly injured one bird that got too close to their hidden entrance. It had wandered off just before Eva and the hunting party had attacked. After checking on the Clan, Eva and the hunting party left to track down the wounded birds. The opportunity to kill three more attackers was too tempting to ignore. Credo led the way.

With great caution, Eva, Credo and the ten warriors moved forward. She gave strict orders for the group to always remain within sight of each other. They soon found the carcass of the first bird. It had a spear embedded in its left flank. They cleaned the bird and buried it in the peat moss. The party then followed the trail of the next wounded animal. Within ten minutes they found it near death. They quickly ran it through with several spears. Now the warriors had killed half of the attacking contingent. The trail of the last wounded bird was being followed. Eva told everyone to hang back as she and Credo moved ahead as fast as she was able.

Taking the lead Eva wanted to follow the last bird to the Terror Bird's new nesting or roosting area. Eva didn't want the large hunting party to alert the wounded animal and prevent its return home. Credo ran ahead but cautiously remained in eye contact with his guardian. After about an hour he suddenly stopped. Ahead was a puff of mist, there were trees and dry brown and new green grass. The small patches of snow normally seen were all gone. The ground was much warmer here than elsewhere, and slow-moving streams were flowing. It was marshy and foggy. Visibility was limited and it was spooky. Eva's intuition told her to be very cautious. She then saw the body. The last wounded bird was laying half in a pool and half out. It wasn't moving. Probably dead. Suddenly two Terror Birds appeared and pushed their dead comrade under the water. They then looked around and ran directly away from where Credo and Eva were watching. They hopped through a gap in some rocks and disappeared.

As if stalking a bison herd, Eva and Credo crept forward. They cautiously went through the gap the birds had negotiated earlier. Once through, the pair hid behind a rock outcrop before proceeding. What they saw before them was a large basin. At the bottom was a lake. On the shoreline were about a dozen Terror Birds attending nests surrounding the small lake. Eva felt this group of birds was likely the entire remaining population.

She immediately signaled Credo to follow her silently and quickly. Her only thought was what to do next? Eva's hunting party was way too small to attack this sanctuary. Even with the element of surprise it would be suicide. She returned to the waiting clansmen and described her findings. It was decided the group would return to the rock pile camp and live to fight another day. They had adequate food and safety there to get them into the Summer and need not challenge the birds until a future time of their choice. This however was not to be. The birds had other ideas. The tribe was soon forced to take a different strategy.

Within the first week of their return, the Terror Birds attacked again. This time neither party lost fighters. However, the birds harassed the Clan every day from that day forward. They never allowed the Clan to get comfortable or let their guard down. It became a war of nerves. Eva was getting uneasy as the temperament of the people was getting nasty. Bickering was continual and fights between families were intensifying. She had to do something.

Eva knew the birds were flightless and were unable to climb trees. They could sometimes reach low hanging limbs by leaping short vertical distances or by using their size and strength to knock down small saplings. Though these amazing animals were physically superior to humans, they did have limitations. Eva was about to take advantage of their lack of agility. She called a meeting and discussed a plan to use the Clan's human abilities to frustrate and possibly eliminate and end the war for good.

The war council added their ideas to the mix. It was a technology the humans had acquired . . . fire, a technology the birds were unable to duplicate. So, armed with these weapons the plan was hatched to go on the offensive. But not until the warriors had tested and perfected their knowledge and techniques. First it was decided to place lookouts high in large trees between the encampment and the bird sanctuary. The lookouts were charged with observing but not attacking.

Platforms were added to the strategy after the initial trees were identified. The warriors notched the trunks and climb them in a matter of seconds. The hunters could reach heights the birds could neither jump to or in many cases even see. Their anatomy limited them to normally see from their height forward, from side to side, in reverse or down. It had been discovered looking up was difficult and disorienting to the birds.

For several weeks the Clan practiced tactics and gathered intelligence on their enemy. To Eva's delight this activity ceased the internal fighting within the Tribe. A common plan and effort supported by all was the solution. It was discovered by their surveillance that the birds sent out two marauders daily. These assailants left before dawn and returned to their sanctuary soon after sundown. It was now time for the humans to take the next step.

Eva took a team of climbers and went to the swamp area near the roost and nesting basin. This was done deep at night to reduce the chance of detection. After climbing to the highest levels possible, a team of observers was left in place. It was hoped that from their height, the observers could see over the rock barrier and into the basin surrounding the small lake. They would know the next morning. At first light all four observers were able to see some portion of the basin. Their reports revealed strategic intelligence.

First, the birds numbered around twenty adults. There were no chicks that could be seen. It was assumed hatching was not yet in progress but would occur by late Spring. This was within a few days from now. Since the birds would be expected to protect the hatchlings, an attack coinciding with this season would be perfectly timed and cause the most damage.

Next, the basin was basically a box canyon. The entrance was their exit. To be blunt, warriors could block the gap with little investment. And then proceed to attack the flock from atop the canyon walls and from trees within the basin. Eva was almost uneasy at the possibilities. She had the plan and people to destroy a species. Could she do what she had been dreaming of doing? To hesitate now might allow the Terror Birds to move elsewhere and escape to fight another round with her Clan.

Eva slept badly all night. Even Credo's purring annoyed her. It was her responsibility to decide whether to attack and she would have to live with her decision. If only she could communicate with these animals. As much as she hated them, Eva admired their strength, speed and beauty. Once gone, she could not bring them back. This was a one-way decision. She woke with a pain in her neck and was agitated and stressed beyond normal. Fear she could handle; however, this state of mind was devastating because it would not leave. No matter her decision, Eva knew she would forever second guess herself. She either fought or left. This location was now home and moving could mean confrontation with another tribe or species they could not defeat. Literally, a bird in the hand was better than two in the bush. The decision was made.

Eva took all but the elderly and those too young to fight. Their number was thirty-two warriors and one saber cat. The battle plan was in Eva's mind, but she knew not to be too rigid. Refusing to change tactics in response to evolving circumstances could lead to disaster. The plan of attack needed to be flexible the minute the fighting began. The enemy seldom cooperated to destroy themselves.

The attack was to begin before the two marauders left for the day. They planned to use fire to block the exit to the basin. This would be started only after all the warriors were in position on top of the canyon walls and in the trees as close to the basin floor as possible. All had torches to light once the fire was started to block the exit. New slings and spears had been manufactured. Each warrior carried twice the number normally deployed. The group climbed on top of the wall and gathered stones, rocks and boulders to rain down on the birds. A double number of the warriors were concentrated near the entrance. Brush, dry grass and other combustibles were stacked in the gap. Eva was on the wall near the entrance with Credo at her side. She sensed everything was as ready as possible. She ordered the fire started and the lighting of all the torches. Once everyone saw the torches, they were to yell at the top of their lungs and attack any moving thing within the basin.

The flames leaped from the entrance and torches glowed all around the basin walls. There was no movement below. The Terror Birds were gone! Eva's plan had failed.

The Boneyard War Continues

Short Story 3
Short Story by George and Linda B

Preface

Eva took all but the elderly and those too young to fight. The plan of attack needed to be flexible the minute the fighting began. The enemy seldom cooperated to destroy themselves.

The attack was to begin before the two marauders left for the day. They planned to use fire to block the exit to the basin. This would be started only after all the warriors were in position on top of the canyon walls and in the trees as close to the basin floor as possible. Eva was on the wall near the entrance with

Credo at her side. She sensed everything was as ready as possible. She ordered the fire started and the lighting of all the torches. Once everyone saw the torches, they were to yell at the top of their lungs and attack any moving thing within the basin. The flames leaped from the entrance and torches glowed all around the basin walls. There was no movement below.

The Terror Birds were gone!

The Boneyard War Continues
Short Story by George and Linda B

Eva was dumbfounded! Her shock was profound. All their plans and effort were made moot. She immediately realized the birds could be assaulting their camp! She signaled Credo, her companion saber cat, to run to the camp immediately. She also sent her fastest warriors; they left the basin as quickly as they could.

The leader of the human Clan had seriously underestimated her enemy. They were not simple, instinct-driven animals. Eva suspected for the first time that the Terror Birds had a leader and that the leader could reason. Since the birds had no audible voice except shrieks, she surmised they used a form of telepathy or directed thoughts. If so, she might be able to intercept such communication, much like she used with Credo, in emergencies when sign language was not possible or efficient.

Eva struggled to keep up with her warriors in the race to return to camp. She had to stop occasionally to rest her leg. A few clansmen hung back to assure she did not get separated from the Tribe. To lose Eva would be a tragedy and would have devastating consequences.

When she was about two thirds of the way back to the camp, Credo met her. To Eva's relief, he was calm, and she knew the encampment was safe.

Upon her arrival, the Clan was gathered. Eva explained what she felt happened at the Basin. She detailed her fear that their enemy was way more intelligent than they assumed. She and Credo, along with a few warriors, would return to the Basin and attempt to track where the Birds went. She asked the camp to stay vigilant, the Birds may be planning retaliation for the humans attempt at genocide. The war council accepted her strategy.

Eva was sleepless, her mind was racing all night. When game was scarce the competition with the Bird Clan was inevitable. Now game is abundant and there is enough for everyone. There is no reason to eradicate the Terror Birds except as a preventative measure. As long as each side saw each other as prey, nothing would change. Eva, decided to attempt a different approach. However, she needed to locate the Bird's roost and discover their plans for her humans.

Credo with Eva and three of the Clan's top trackers left together. They went to the Basin first and searched for clues to indicate the direction the Terror Birds took. After several false alerts, Credo was the one who was able to detect the correct trail. Circling in larger and larger arcs he ignored the first scent trails. Credo knew the first trails were laid down to misdirect trackers. It appeared the Birds had finally consolidated their group and to Eva's astonishment they were headed toward the Boneyard. Why?

Then it made sense. Eva realized the Boneyard neutralized the advantages the Clan had over the Terror Birds at the Basin. Within the Boneyard there were no trees, so the humans could not avoid direct attack by the charging birds. Fires would be totally ineffective because there were no combustibles to ignite and finally, visibility was extremely limited. At the Boneyard the two enemies were on equal ground!

This reality gave the advantage to the Bird Clan. Eva could not even contemplate an all-out assault on them within the mist laden and maze-like territory. This area sported dozens of boiling pools of colored algae and sulfur laden thermals. A coordinated and aggressive group in place within this natural fortress was almost impossible to successfully defeat.

Eva realized the Birds retreated to this haven because they had little choice. Her Clan's rockpile was now equivalent to the Bird Clan's Boneyard. Both within striking distance of each other, but both truly unassailable. They were now at a true stalemate. Neither dared to eliminate the other without unacceptable consequences. Eva almost laughed out loud at the situation! She needed a totally new strategy to deal with her new state of affairs.

Raven, the leader of the Bird Clan was angry he had lost so many of his species. The battle with this small band of humans had been disastrous. He had lost half of his Tribe and was in no better position now than when the war started last summer. At that time, game was scarce due to the drought, and the humans were a direct competitor for the available food. Raven thought they could kill the humans for much needed food while removing them as competing apex predators. All his strategies and ploys had failed. The humans were not as easy to scare or outthink as were the wolf packs. They must have a strong and intelligent leader. His decision to return to the Boneyard was an act of desperation after he realized the Brooding Basin had become a self-made trap that almost ended in total annihilation.

Eva was sleeping as was now her custom on top of the rock pile. She had been occasionally successful in visualizing in her dreams a Terror Bird with a plume of jet-black feathers on his crown. She intuitively knew he was the Bird Clan Leader. She called him Raven. Her feeling about Raven was extreme caution tempered with an intense curiosity. She knew he was an intellectual match to any creature she had encountered. Now she knew who outsmarted her at the Brooding Basin assault failure. He was no fool, but neither was she.

It was apparent to both Eva and Raven they were in a Mexican standoff. Who was to make the first move to change the battlefield? Eva was the first to act. She placed observers in trees at the extreme entrances and exits of the Boneyard. This strategy was more difficult than she first thought because of the enormity of the thermal populated area. However, because of the natural barriers and topography, the observers soon realized there were only six routes in and out of the yard that were routinely used.

Eva soon discovered the Bird Clan's weakness. The Birds could not kill prey and bring large pieces of it back to their roost. They could only eat their fill at the time and place of their kill and would regurgitate portions of it for their chicks or other adults. This weakness meant they had to hunt and kill more often than humans. It also meant the Birds had to hunt in groups of three or less to sustain their higher rate of kills.

Armed with this knowledge Eva had a larger group of her people shadow a smaller Bird hunting party and pounce on them as they were trying to eat their kill. This practice went on for several weeks. Thus, taking the Birds' hard-earned prey and feeding the humans with extra food while slowly starving the Birds.

Raven was seeing his clansmen weaken. His most successful hunting parties were being harassed at higher and higher rates. Though prey was abundant their easy access to it was greatly restricted. He had long given up on attacking the human camp because it was almost immune to their efforts. He had to set a trap for them. But what?

He knew the humans selected only one hunting party each day to shadow and harass. So, this time he would wait to see which one they followed. Soon he would have all the hunters not followed by the humans return immediately to the Boneyard and form a war party to confront the human thieves from their rear. He would attack in mass the unsuspecting and hopefully outnumbered humans.

Eva was uneasy for some reason, though her plan to combat the Terror Birds was working flawlessly. She warned her marauding team to never allow themselves to be trapped in a situation where a larger number of birds could out flank or surround them without recourse. She had them strategize how to react to such a situation.

The confrontation between the two species came one day in mid-summer. Eva and Credo were tagging along on this day. Eva had a nightmare the previous night and knew to expect something new. She remembered dreaming Raven led a large group of Terror Birds in an ambush on a group of her hunters. She was mentally ready.

Though she was strong and healthy, her leg prevented her from keeping pace with the faster hunting party. So, she lagged behind with Credo by her side. Eva kept an eye on trees she could negotiate quickly to limit an easy attack from a group of Terror Birds. The same tactic she instilled in her clansmen. While her leg was a problem, she could still negotiate the same tree haven Credo could; one that was slanted. Together they could hold off several attackers coming from only one direction.

Eva and Credo sensed danger simultaneously. The hair on her neck stiffened. She immediately surveyed her surroundings. The clansmen were in front of her and were out of sight and voice contact as well. This left the impending danger behind her. She spotted a tree that had been partially uprooted and hanging over a deep gorge. She and Credo scrambled quickly aboard. She had a clear shot at anything approaching the base of the leaning tree.

Eva first saw them as black figures moving over a ridge behind her. She counted over a dozen or more. The Clan's hunting party ahead was only six in number. A one on one assault at ground level would be disastrous for the humans.

Though Eva was in clear sight, she sensed they had not yet detected either her or Credo. Eva then saw Raven. He was the largest of them all, probably nine feet tall and weighing six hundred pounds. His black crown plume further distinguished him from the rest.

She and Credo were no match for even two of this group if on even turf. However, with the element of surprise and her ability to keep out of their reach, Eva could cause them substantial delay and difficulty. She decided to act. She allowed the two lead birds to pass by and hoped Raven was at the lead of their war party. To her surprise he appeared like magic within one hundred yards of her. Eva readied the best stone she had in her sling. She steadied herself and calculated the closing distance. The windup included circling the stone burdened sling over her head several times. When she released the stone, it was at its maximum velocity and perfect vector. Her effort almost dislodged her from her perch.

The stone zoomed with deadly speed toward her target. As luck would have it, Raven stopped abruptly. One of his lieutenants stepped in front of him and took the full force of the projectile to his right temple. He died instantly. Raven, saw a tiny female human and Credo within thirty yards of him. He eyed her and his fallen clansman. He turned with a shriek and retreated with his entire party, knowing his sneak attack was now discovered and a failure.

Eva could not believe her eyes. Knowing them not to be cowards, she concluded Raven suspected an ambush to his ambush was awaiting them. She could not believe her good fortune. After some time, she and Credo dismounted the tree and began to clean and butcher the dead bird. Within two hours the Clan's six-member hunting party returning home met up with her. They were dragging tree limbs upon which was the butchered carcass of a freshly killed elk they took from the Terror Birds. They now assisted Eva and loaded the Terror Bird on the drag. All and all this day was a great day for the humans and a doubly bad one for the Birds.

Raven was stunned. How did the humans know his plan? Their leader must be an old and wise male. The young female that killed his lieutenant must have been an expendable underling. A rear guard left to die for the benefit of their people. In his long memory, these humans were the most difficult, stubborn and ruthless enemy he had ever faced. From this terrible day forward, Raven sent out a minimum of six hunters in a party. This reduced their opportunity to kill prey but guaranteed what they killed they could eat.

Eva, realizing Raven's change in strategy, did not challenge a pod of six Terror Birds. She felt to do so required at least twelve of her best clansmen. The risk of losing people going against these odds was prohibitive. The two warring parties returned to a relative stalemate; however, the humans now had established they were the dominant party in the war.

Winter was quickly approaching and neither Clan had attacked or harassed each other for some time. Both were preparing for the upcoming bitter winter in the best way they knew how. In fact, both groups knew the hunting patterns of the other and avoided any possible conflicts. An unofficial truce evolved between the two parties. But then something quite unexpected and new happened. The two groups began to focus on the same bison and elk herds, though from two different directions and techniques. They found out quite by accident that the activities of one Clan could easily assist the other with their hunting efficiency. And more and more this coincidence kept happening. Thus, both Clans mutually benefited from each other's efforts. This was not lost on Eva or Raven. They understood the implications.

One day a large human party stumbled across a smaller Bird party eating a downed bison. The humans did not rush the Birds and steal their prey. They simply, slowly and visually bypassed the Birds and their prize. Soon after a small child had wandered off from the human encampment. When the parents and a search party tracked down the toddler it was noted two Terror Birds had been within easy killing distance of the lost child and had not harmed it in any way. Eva knew this situation was probably only temporary and was a direct result of the abundance of game for both Clans. The real test would come when competition for food became an issue again.

Raven had also noted the difference in the hunting activities and interaction between the two Clans. He welcomed the relative truce but was always apprehensive and curious about who was the human leader. He had his suspicions but could never feel certain he was correct. He hoped someday to discern who it could be. He was confident the opportunity would come, and it did, because of an unexpected act of kindness. Later, Raven's trust toward the human leader would grow exponentially as they fought a mutual enemy that could have destroyed both Clans.

This common threat was frightening, coming out of nowhere and without equal. The giant red-haired humanoids were a scourge everywhere they traveled. They were always looking for new hunting grounds because their need for food was enormous. They were violently attacked by any human bands they neared because they fed on the humans as choice prey. Since they appeared to be humans themselves, they were considered cannibals by the smaller subspecies. Gorgee, the family leader, was thirteen feet tall, and weighed 1200 pounds. His strength was enormous. He could easily throw a one-hundred-pound rock fifty yards with one of his six fingered hands. These beings had two rows of teeth and any one of them stunk like a large family of mad skunks. The odor factor was the only characteristic that gave their prey a chance of avoiding their attacks. Gorgee's family unit had a total of ten individuals. There were maybe five such families within an entire country size area. These families were all genetically related but had to separate to find enough food to sustain themselves. One family could kill and eat an entire bison herd within a few weeks. Everywhere they went they brought violence, fear, and starvation. They were the apex of apex predators and nothing stood in their way. Unfortunately, they were on their way toward the Boneyard.

These enormous humanoids called themselves The Immortals. The humans called them Red-Skunk Giants. Gorgee, like his fellow travelers was arrogant and disdainful of all life, including his own people. He and the other giants felt invincible and as a group they were filled with pride which led them to use only the crudest weapons. With their size, strength and speed they were no match to any animal, except for possibly a mammoth or giant land sloth.

Eva had several nightmares over the last several months about a coming challenge. She had dreams of two technical improvements regarding their weapons but did not fully understand what she was see-ing. One appeared to be a tree sapling that had been bent into a bow with a thin rawhide strap holding the two opposing ends. A stick with feathers on one end and a pointed rock attached to the other was launched forward with amazing speed and force. She tried to make such a device but had been frustrated by several issues. The other was a short stick with a small hook on one end and was used to throw spears harder, faster and further than ever before. It basically extended the user's arm from six to ten inches. This one she was able to construct and even got some of her clansmen to practice with it. They drilled a small hole in the blunt end of the spear to insert the crude hook from the throwing or spear lever. This lever laid under the hilt of the spear until it was launched. After numerous trials, her people were able to bring down bison and elk at much longer distances than ever before.

Her dreams were repeated multiple times and she began to realize the rawhide strips needed to be as thin as possible and tightly twisted. After hundreds of attempts she was able to duplicate a few primitive attempts at launching the short stick with the rock attached to the front. In one dream she saw the gut tissue and sinew from animals being twisted into thinner and stronger bow strings. They were also able to use the same string material when applied wet to bind the arrow heads to the short wooden shafts. They found ways to manufacture standard sized arrows in length and diameter. The bow and arrow were being quickly improved because a change could be quickly tested and tweaked and then tested again.

There were several advantages to this novel weapon. It allowed the Clan to hunt more efficiently smaller animals such as squirrels, rabbits and waterfowl. In addition, if a target was missed the arrow was easier to find than a favorite sling stone. The distance at which the arrows were accurate was amazing and could be perfected by more hunters than the slings. Lastly, a target struck by an arrow was more likely to succumb to its wounds than that of a sling stone. However, Eva still preferred the sling over the new weapon. The bow was bulky and required much more preparation. It was also affected by the wind and weather conditions much more than the sling stone. In addition, once all the arrows were expended the bow was almost useless as a weapon. It was like swinging a small tree limb at an adversary. Also, the arrows were limited in number. However, if a hunter ran out of sling stones, finding one on the ground was almost certain. The solution was to add both the bow and arrows and spear lever to the clansmen's existing weapons. The added weight was not enough to cause a problem. However, the bulky items did affect the hunter's agility.

Raven was aware the humans were experimenting with new weapons and noticed their hunting success was dramatically improving. This was a concern, but he was powerless to do anything about their progress. Eva had a dream in which the Terror Birds were hit with some type of illness and were getting weaker and weaker. She decided therefore to offer something to demonstrate her good will. She along with some clansmen dragged a large elk they had killed to the edge of the Boneyard. Raven appeared at the edge of the mist and watched as they left the prey and moved off to a significant distance. Several Terror Birds eventually appeared out of the fog and started to tear at the elk carcass. Raven walked toward the humans without escort and stopped within easy weapon's distance. Eva, with Credo, did likewise. The trio came within a few yards of each other. Eva was amazed at Raven's enormous size and the beauty of his plumage. Raven raised his head and shrieked loudly. The clansmen started to rush forward, and Eva signaled them to remain where they were. Raven then realized this tiny crippled female was the leader of the humans. He was amazed by her bravery. He now remembered when she and Credo took on his entire war party. He put one leg behind the other and bowed his head. Eva returned the gesture in the same manner. Raven then turned and went toward the elk. Eva returned to her clansmen and they left the edge of the Boneyard.

Raven observed the ease at which the humans moved their killed prey to their people. Something his Clan could not do. In his culture, the hunter that provided the most food was the most honored. As cooperation between the Bird Clan and the humans increased, one or more Bird Clansmen accompanied each human hunting party. It was found that his people could carry or drag several hundred pounds of meat for long distances much more efficiently than several humans.

As the trust between the Birds and Eva's Clan increased, the humans fashioned halters which the Terror Birds could easily slip over their necks. These leather inventions made everything easier, including securing large butchered game animals to the halters for easy carry. For their cooperation the humans gave the Birds half of all game taken in their group efforts. Wearing these halters became a thing of pride and position amongst the Bird Tribe. Raven wore one himself as the largest, strongest and highest honored of his Clan.

Weeks after the Boneyard meeting the dreaded day occurred. The giant humanoids arrived looking for game. The odor was the first thing both the Terror Birds and humans noticed. The wind direction made everyone know something was not the same as the day before. Noting the direction from which the smell was coming, Eva sent Credo to investigate while she followed with a couple of clansmen. Raven did almost the identical thing. Since the Terror Birds were much quicker than the humans, they were the first to encounter the invaders. Raven was the first to see the band of giants. They were grouped together in a tight circle. They were gorging on several bison. Each giant had their own carcass. They quickly devoured the bison raw including its bones, leaving only the hide and the horns of the dispatched animals. It looked like the bison had their necks broken and heads twisted off. The group was loudly arguing with each other and if one had not eaten his meal quick enough another giant would attempt to grab what was left of the other's animal. The largest of the group of about ten individuals backhanded two of the ones fighting and yelled with a voice so loud Raven's internal organs shook.

Eva had the two in her party to climb trees to look for the location of the noise. Her intuition was telling her to get no closer. The odor was so strong she was getting nauseous. The two observers almost fell out of the trees when they saw the group of Giants. Comparing the relative size of the two species, the clansmen realized that the nine-foot Raven was small in comparison to the Giants. This was a nightmare. The only solace was these beings appeared to be humans though enormous in size. However, their group behavior quickly made it apparent these beings were not to be approached as potential allies or welcomed visitors. Suddenly, the largest turned with lightning speed and amazing quickness for something of his size and attacked the Terror Birds. Raven quickly side stepped the assault. However, one of his companions was not as lucky. Gorgee grabbed the legs of the bird and tore them apart in one movement. Raven along with his remaining comrade fled the area with all the speed they could muster.

Eva did not have to see what her lookouts were watching. She immediately signaled her people to retreat. Her intuition told her this was a danger far worse than the Terror Birds or even the drought that starved half of her Clan the year before. They were in survival mode for the human and the bird Clans as well. This will take a total effort from everyone just to survive.

On returning to the encampment, Eva held a group council. She told them of her fears and warned them these beasts had no compassion or understanding of other species. From this day forward the Clan erased all evidence of their existence that was possible. Everyone moved deeper into the rock pile. A special effort was made to dig alternate exits from their footholds within the rocks. Total effort was made to place scouts as high in the canopy as possible and Eva developed a system of alerts that everyone understood. Arrows covered in different colors were used for this purpose. They were silent and vocal alerts were prohibited. Piles and cashes of combustible materials were located and supplemented. While the Giants knew about fire, they appeared never to use it. They ate everything raw. This could be a very important fact.

Credo and Eva went out by themselves. Her nose and her intuition told her where the skunk smelling humanoids were located. She and Credo found an observation perch and watched the beasts for hours. She realized neither the Bird Clan nor her people could hunt while the things were present. Her Tribe had to leave, starve or fight and they probably couldn't leave without being hunted down and eaten in the process. This was the easiest decision she ever made. They would fight. But how?

While observing the Giants, Eva discovered some things that could be used to defeat these enormous humanoids. First, they had no true cohesion or loyalty. The biggest Skunk that seemed to be their leader was one they appeared to call Gorgee. The group feared but did not respect or honor him. Gorgee yelled and used physical abuse to enforce his orders. They were afraid of being shunned or exiled from the group or family. The Giant's weapons were crude stone for the most part. They had something that resembled a spear, but it was not tipped with a sharp stone. The weapon was just the smaller end of a straight tree trunk. Their clothes were a bit more sophisticated. They might have been even woven by someone or made by some technology Eva had not seen before. It was as though these beings had access to better technologies but chose to do without it or were not allowed to use it by some higher power.

Her first thought was they needed to isolate one of the family and dispatch, injure or scare it to death. The plan would be to lure one or more of them away from the rest and complete the plan. Eva and Credo went to the Boneyard and stood at the outer limits of the mist clouds. Raven soon appeared. Eva pointed toward the Giant's camp; then pointed toward the Brooding Basin. She then passed her hand across her throat. Next, she pointed to the sun twice. Raven bowed and returned into the fog.

For two days the Clan made the same preparations they had made for the Terror Birds when they had attempted to trap and exterminate the Birds within their box canyon, Eva called this area the Brooding Basin. The walls were almost vertical and were at least one hundred feet high. The gap in the walls was in one place and could easily be blocked by a large fire. The humans could place themselves on the canyon walls and in the tall trees around the small lake in the basin. From these perches they could launch arrows, sling stones, fire and boulders. The Terror Birds that were to lead the Skunk Giants into the canyon would be augmented by at least a dozen more Terror Birds hiding within. The number and locations of the Birds hidden was up to Raven.

Before sunrise on the third morning, Eva with Credo walked to the edge of the Boneyard. Raven came to Eva and sat down by her side. He lowered his head and grunted. Using the halter, he was wearing, She took the hint and climbed upon his back.

Though her leg limited Eva's ability to move quickly and maintain command, her position on Raven's back ended these limitations. She, Raven, Credo and four other Terror Birds with clansmen riders headed for the Giant's camp. The Terror Birds with their human riders standing tall were approaching the height of the Giants. The human riders had long spears, bows, and hatchets. Raven and Eva topped the ridge above the Giant's camp. They were sleeping as it was just before sunrise. Eva had the riders dismount and creep as close to the sleeping Giants as they dare.

On her command the riders took their bows and shot as many arrows as possible into the sleeping bodies. They remounted, lit torches and formed up and headed toward Raven and Eva. Of the ten Giants, surprisingly three never lived to rise. Two more were wounded significantly and could not chase the riders into the dark. The rest followed the torches into the night. Credo then attacked the two left in the camp. He quickly killed one and left the other more injured than when he began. Credo then followed behind the trailing Giants.

As the insanely angry Gorgee ran toward the torches in the distance, he felt fear. It was disorienting. He never thought anyone would attack them successfully. When something like this happened before they had never lost any of their family. He thought they were not able to be killed. In the past all such attackers were always immediately hunted down and mercilessly tortured before they were eaten alive. He intended to do the same to these devils as soon as possible no matter what it cost him.

The Terror Birds were very fast, but Eva had them stay close enough that the Giants never lost visual contact with the torches. As the sun rose the torches were no longer needed and the five just stayed out of the Giants' attack distance . . .assuming it was somewhere around one hundred yards.

As Raven and Eva approached the gap in the rock walled canyon of the Brooding Basin they stopped. The four mounted companions leaped through the opening. Eva wanted to make sure the Giants had no trouble seeing them enter the basin. They waited and when Eva saw Gorgee, she slung a stone directly at him. It struck him on his chest, and he wrenched with pain. She yelled and smiled broadly. Raven shrieked with joy. Gorgee cursed and ran forward encouraging his four companions on without caution. They entered the gap and ran into the basin. After the Giants entered, the Clan moved brush, dried grass and other dry wood to the entrance and lit it immediately. The Clan had collected leather bags of pitch from pools near the Boneyard and threw them on the flames as well. The entrance quickly became a furnace.

While the fire was building, the five riders were forming up on the opposite side of the lake. The Giants rushed forward and halted near the shore. Gorgee screamed with anger as he looked with rage at the Terror Birds and humans across the water. Eva responded with a high-toned yell. Raven shrieked with three bursts, each louder than the one before. The humans returned Eva's yell from the canyon walls and from the trees within the basin. Repeating the same yell Raven made two dozen Terror Birds appeared from the brush near the canyon walls and moved forward. Gorgee was stunned and his cursing stopped, his heart fluttered hard in his chest. He turned and ran for the entrance. Their enemy allowed them to proceed as far as they wished. The heat was so intense once they passed the first rock outcrop the lead Giant's clothing ignited. She ran from the gap on fire and jumped into the lake. Gorgee and the rest returned to the basin and picked up stones or anything else they could use as a weapon. A most foolish Giant threw a large stone toward Raven and Eva. Raven with Eva mounted on his back simply sidestepped the projectile. The thrower was struck almost simultaneously by two dozen arrows and fell dead in seconds. Gorgee fell to his knees screaming and covered his face with his hands. He knew he was at the mercy of these beings from the Boneyard. Eva, had to think fast. Was there any reason to spare the lives of the four remaining Giants? She had no desire to turn them into prisoners. She couldn't even afford to keep them fed. Nor did she want to free them to prey on other Clans or animal herds. She could release one or more to warn other Giant families to stay away from the Boneyard or she could kill them all. Turning to Raven she gave him the decision to do what he felt necessary. Raven remembered the way his lieutenant was ripped apart like a toy by Gorgee and he didn't even blink. He gave the order to attack and the Terror Birds rushed the surviving Giants. Within two minutes the Giants were shredded into pieces and all that was left was the horrible odor.

The bodies of the Giants were left to be scavenged by whatever animals wished to graze on them, that is, the ones that could stand the smell. In months the Clan would collect the bleached bones of these monsters and placed them in the Boneyard with the other animals that had died there. The wounded red headed Giant that Credo left alive recovered enough from his injuries, crawled off and eventually found another family. He told them of his experience and the loss of Gorgee and the rest of his family. The new family, listened and then quickly killed the coward. They left his body for the worms that could stand the odor.

A golden age persisted for several seasons in and around the Boneyard. Both the Rock Pile Human Clan and the Terror Bird Clan continued to cooperate and thrive. The connection and mutual respect between Raven and Eva became a given fact. The two Clans were the uncontested rulers of the Boneyard and the thousands of square miles around it.

They Painted her Face

Short Story 4
By George and Linda B

Thankful to be alive, Eva thought: *I raged against* the *odds . . . but I prevailed for some purpose.* She thoroughly understood her history and present status. Eva's parents struggled to protect her from the normal course of events that befell such a child. Her clubbed foot made her life tenuous. Most children born with such deformities were placed on a hill and allowed to die. Her parents refused to do so and thus were initially treated as near outcasts. Even now Eva in her late teens and the uncontested leader of her Clan, felt the residual burden of the past. How this happened was hard to explain, she didn't try because her duties made it almost impossible to worry about the past.

No one challenged her position in the Tribe, though not a tyrant, she did not have friends. The Chief never did because of the necessity to maintain absolute neutrality. Life and death decisions came with the territory and perceived favoritism in exercising such authority would quickly lead to disaster. This unfortunately contributed to the death of her parents. When the great drought resulted in the Tribe's relocation now several cycles past the weak and injured clansmen were left behind to fend for themselves.

Though she did not have evidence her parents died, it was an absolute certainty they had perished because they would have joined the Clan at the Boneyard long before now. It was possible that one of the few friendly Clans might have wandered through and found those they had to leave behind. This possibility, however, was remote because the migrating Clans were probably in the same or a worse situation than they had been. These Clans occasionally camped together and sometimes men and women would marry one or another and leave with or join with the visiting Tribe. Thus, extended families existed across these groups.

Before the famine years ago, Eva's parents were the healers and her mother the midwife of the Tribe. Thus, the Tribe allowed a certain amount of latitude to them regarding her protection as she grew up. The previous leader had looked upon her parents and Eva with disdain and mistrust. He had eventually become very hateful and abusive towards them though they were the most beneficial members of the Clan.

As Eva grew from early childhood, the Tribe had experienced many seasons of plenty, so food resources and minor accommodations regarding her handicap were readily tolerated. She seldom played with the other children because her foot made such normal activities difficult. However, when it was discovered Eva had talents and capabilities no one else had, everyone forgot about her deformity. Her intuition was well developed even as a small child. She would correctly warn her people that weather conditions were about to change, and precautions should be made. She guided the hunters where game was more abundant and gave them advice on how to position themselves to be most successful. Hunting parties would often carry her with them on their backs. On these adventures Eva was her happiest.

Her love for the Clan grew and the Clan for her increased daily. Her reputation for helping the Tribe was without question. Because of her intelligence and wisdom, she was sought to adjudicate minor disagreements, her ability to solve even complex situations was a continual surprise.

As she grew with Credo by her side, she learned from everyone. Her mother instructed her, and she assisted in childbirth. Her father taught her the healing skills and how to identify herbs and prepare treatments and set bones and other life saving techniques. She learned how to make weapons and perfected her ability to make and use the sling. Despite Eva's small size and stature, she became the most accurate and deadly of all the clansmen, and further taught Credo how to assist in the hunt by driving game toward a trap. Between them they developed a language. She used hand signals and he responded with grunts and other vocalizations.

Eva sensed the jealousy and hatred the Clan Chief had toward her and her parents. This came to a head when her father was searching for medicinal herbs and found the den of a saber cat. Within it he found the mother and three kits. The mother was dead as were two of her three offspring. Eva's father took the juvenile with him. He brought it back to the camp and Eva latched on to the small fur ball immediately. She worked tirelessly to keep the animal alive. She named him Credo. The Clan Chief wanted the young animal removed from the camp and eliminated. He confronted Eva's parents and demanded they comply with his wishes. In an extremely rare event, her father refused, and the Clan members united to defy the Chief's desire. Everyone felt the young animal would eventually get lost, die of natural causes or have a lethal accident. However, he thrived though blind in one eye. Credo slowly became the camp mascot along with Eva and the Tribal Leader became politically diminished as a result.

This low-level warfare continued throughout Eva's childhood and ended with the death of the Chief. The Clan Leader was the son of the previous Chief and as was expected his son would succeed him upon his death. The Tribal leader's son was inept and incompetent. He was the least capable hunter and provider in the Clan. He made himself an enemy to all within the Tribe; he used his position to get his way even when it was not warranted. The only thing he was good at was being a bully and a thief.

As fate would have it, the Leader was badly injured in an accident on a hunting trip. He was attacked by a bull elk and had multiple injuries. His son's cowardice contributed to or even caused his injuries and the rest of the hunting party knew this. On return Eva's Father did all he could to save the man's life, but the injuries were too severe. He died within a few days and after the mourning period a new leader was to be named. The selection was done by a group of the five oldest members of the Clan. Within the group were two women and three men.

At sunrise the Chief's son stood in front of the camp with the common fire separating him from the rest of the people. He stood there anticipating having his face painted by the eldest member of the Tribe.

Everyone in the Clan, young and old were there. He stood by himself with his back straight and his head high looking over the fire at the assembled people. The old man took the red ochre in his leather pouch and was to paint a red line under the eyes and across the bridge of the nose of the new chief. Then he was to paint six red blotches under the line, three on each side. The seventh red mark was to be added below the lower lip on the chin. These marks were symbolic of the truths handed down to the Elders from their ancestors. They were to remind all that saw them, the person wearing them was the chosen guardian and voluntary servant to the Tribe. The red marks were for wisdom, honesty, devotion, compassion, courage, and honor. The line below the eyes was to enable clear vision providing neutrality and justice. The mark below the lips was to prevent any words that contained deceit from coming forth.

As all were watching, the old man hesitated. He then turned to look behind him at the entire assembled Clan, then turned to his left allowing the other four Elders to walk forward with someone small behind them. When they were near the Common Fire they parted, Eva walked forward with her face painted with the Clan Leader's markings.

The Chief's son, yelled from the opposite side of the fire. "They painted her face!" In utter disbelief and outrage he raised his spear to kill Eva. That was the last sound he made. Three spears struck him in the chest. He died in his rage.

Eva's constant companion, family and protector was a large saber cat. None of the men in the Clan approached not only because she was the Clan leader but because the custom of her people was that anyone with a deformity was not allowed to marry and have children. If this were not true, she would have been courted, married and probably would have already had at least one child. Because of her bond with Credo, and their similar life spans, the two were a matched pair until their death sometime in the future.

The Clan was now in a golden era. Their numbers had grown from around sixty starving individuals to well over three hundred well fed clansmen. They no longer moved from one location to another chasing game and seasons. They had put down roots near the outskirts of the Boneyard near a landslide or rockpile from which they took their name… The Rockpile Clan. Eva had befriended a near-by clan the Boneyard Tribe and the symbiotic relationship between the two made their lives equally beneficial. Raven was the leader of the Boneyard Clan and he and Eva often were found together surveying the hunting grounds of their territory. Since their victory over the Red Headed Giant Families, the combined forces of Eva and Raven had not been challenged.

With Raven's ability to cover enormous distances, they would camp in one centralized location where Credo would bed down and Raven with Eva on his back would cover fifty miles in one day. Eva did not know when a challenge would occur, but she had recently become apprehensive. This tension was getting more and more intense with each excursion.

Eva had heard stories from the Elders about the size and strength of mammoths but had never seen one. This was to change today. She and Raven were at the far eastern end of their hunting grounds in an area where large bison and elk herds often grazed in the spring. The two just topped a tall ridge and below them was a massive herd of the giants. As far as she could see the wooly beasts meandered, there were probably over a thousand of them grazing below. While she was mesmerized by their presence, Eva was calculating the meaning of what she was witnessing. What did this mean to Raven's and her peoples? These beasts were pushing over trees and altering pools, ponds, and stream courses. They were bursting through beaver dams and altering the very environment that supported fish, waterfowl and other game animals. If these animals remained in the area it would take decades to recover from their presence. Just when things were bad, it suddenly got worse. She was so concentrated on the giant's behavior she had not noticed the humans following the herd and the dogs that were with them.

Suddenly a spear zoomed past her head and immediately she became aware of the humans and heard the dogs howl. A group of five or six warriors were rushing her position and several large dogs were in front of the group. Raven reversed his position and Eva almost fell off his back. The nine-foot flightless bird launched his 650 pounds down the ridge more than forty-five miles an hour. Within seconds the two were in the tree line on the other side of the valley and well out of the reach of the attacking group. From the cover of the trees on the next ridge Eva and Raven watched the humans and dogs search the area they were just in. One of the dogs was able to pick up the scent but his master seeing the direction the trail was going ordered the dog to cease the chase. There was a brief meeting of the attack party and two men with one dog started to follow their trail. This was to Eva's liking; the odds were now better. Eva had her sling, bone hatchet and a bow and arrows. Though she preferred her sling, the bow was a much more lethal weapon at longer distances. If Credo was with them, she would be in the superior tactical position. She and Raven watched as the two men closed the distance getting closer and closer. They had the dog controlled with a leather lead. This canine became more and more agitated as the scent got stronger. Eva was fascinated by their use of the dog. She had never seen this before. So instead of retreating she stayed to watch the behavior of the three approaching them.

To her surprise the two men stopped and then released the dog. He lunged toward their position. Eva instinctively grabbed her sling and launched a stone toward the attacking animal. The dog was struck on his right flank and fell immediately yelping with pain. She did not intend to kill the animal, wanting only to incapacitate him temporarily. However, the dog did not even try to get up. The men seeing their animal downed lifted their spears but had no real idea where the stone had come or that even a stone had injured or killed their animal. They quickly retreated leaving the downed dog assuming it to be dead.

After the men had gone, Eva and Raven left the cover of the trees and went to the prostrate canine. The animal was breathing but otherwise unresponsive. It looked to weigh about eighty pounds and could have easily killed her or a small man without much effort. She examined the animal and determined it had a few broken ribs and a badly injured front leg. She tied the animal's legs together and hung it from Raven's leather halter. She fashioned a leather loop and made a makeshift collar she could tighten with the remaining length of a leather strap (a choke collar). The three left for the Camp to get Credo.

On their trip back to the Boneyard, Eva was fascinated about what she had seen. This new human Clan had obviously trained canines to hunt and work for them. It also appeared that the humans were following mammoths, but the mammoths were not fleeing from them. She was amazed at their cooperation with the canines and even more fascinated by their interaction with the mammoths.

Once they had returned to the Rockpile the dog had gained its consciousness and was in pain but ate and drank. It easily accepted Eva, Credo and Raven as its new pack. This amazed Eva. Never had she seen an animal so easily modify its allegiance to new companions as readily. She named him Limp. It was a good name because he would probably always have a slight limp in his right front leg because of her attack. Both Clans were dumbfounded by Limp because up to now all canines were just wolfs. The only thing they knew about them was to be afraid of them or should kill them.

Eva's family now had a new member. Limp warmed up immediately to Eva and even Credo. His sense of smell and ability to track game was phenomenal. He was integrated into the life of the Clan smoothly. The mammoths quickly exited along with their human handlers but left their destruction. Many spawning areas for fish and nesting areas for waterfowl were totally devastated. Eva was concerned but she now had a reprieve at least until they passed through again. Next time she hoped they would be more prepared for their appearance. However, she wondered if the bison and elk herds could be managed or approached in the same way the mammoths allowed. This was a significant question she wished to answer.

Within the camp, now more correctly called a village, was a thriving mecca of activity. The structures housing the Tribe were now not just temporary tents of sticks and hides but were combinations of stones and timber with sod roofs. Baskets and pottery were being manufactured. The arrows and bows were being expertly refined. The Terror Birds were nesting within the confines of the village especially during hatching season and the bond between humans and birds was getting more sophisticated. The feathered clansmen were choosing human families to align themselves with. Both species went on every hunting party together. The birds became the transportation and the heavy lifters. The humans used their more efficient weapons and tools to bring the game down, cleaned and butchered the prey and paid the birds with half of the kill. Both species benefited from the relationships. There was a form of friendship created between man and bird, typified by the one between Eva and Raven.

The Terror birds paired for life between male and female. Raven's mate or his Queen named "Jewel" had been with him for twenty years. The two of them now lived within Eva's compound. Since Raven was nine feet tall, Eva had an open structure built specifically for Raven and his Queen with a very high ceiling that dominated the village. Eva's primary duties were maintaining a group of warriors and mounts that guarded the limits of their hunting grounds. Mounted on Raven's back Eva would spend half of her time out on the security rounds. That is how she encountered the Mammoth Herders months ago and procured Limp. One of their duties was to keep an eye on the elk and bison herds to protect them from extreme predation i.e. from wolf packs and hostile human groups. When her security troops appeared most predators (animal or human) immediately retreated. Occasionally a large human group would try to invade their territory and it would take a show of force to discourage them. So far there had not been a death or injury on either side of the potential confrontations. This was about to change.

The Fanatics

Short Story 5
By George and Linda B

Eva and Raven were patrolling to the extreme north of their territory. The limits of this area were bounded by a significant river that usually contained large sections of unfordable whitewater. She and Raven targeted this specific location because this was the one place where an easy crossing could be made. They found a very large group of people camped on the far side. From their view they estimated an encampment that numbered in the hundreds. The smoke from the cooking fires alone was so thick that it was hard to see the entire group clearly. There was no doubt this camp was there for a reason. Eva could hear dogs barking and rhythmic drums beating. Her intuition was in high gear. The scene made the hair stand up on the back of her neck. She knew this was a major threat.

The warrior and bird mounts with them were instructed to return to the Boneyard and alert every person able to defend their home territory. Time was important because once the invaders were over the river it would be much more difficult to repel them. Limp was accompanying Raven and Eva, but Credo was back at the Yard. He had a mate now and was living with his family in the wilderness on the far side of the Boneyard Thermals. He occasionally came to the Rockpile village to visit but that had become less and less frequent.

The three bedded down for the night and Eva did not sleep well at all. She had not been this upset for several cycles. She kept hearing things from across the river that disturbed her. There were yells and screams not known to her or her people. She had interacted with several human clans over the years but this one was distinctive and disturbing. The next morning there were three human bodies hanging from the trees along the river.

Did these humans know she was on the other side of the water? Was this a warning for an invasion or was this their normal behavior? If these bodies be psychological warfare, it was working. Eva was spooked. Two days after the bodies were seen, several dugout canoes were being readied to cross the river. Eva prayed her reinforcements would arrive before the primitive crafts were launched. It would only take a few minutes for them to reach her side of the river.

A group of warriors, all men with painted bodies and shaved heads gathered on the opposite shore. They started with a war chant. It grew louder and louder. A ram's horn was blown several times and the men jumped into the canoes. She estimated the number to be about fifty in the first wave. However, behind them were enough to fill the canoes several times. All and all she estimated probably three hundred frenzied warriors. Their weapons were very long spears, large knives and hatchets. To her relief they did not appear to possess bows, nor did they seem to have spear levers either. The canoes also carried a few canines. She didn't think they would be willing to negotiate. Eva had no doubt they were violent invaders. Quickly she did a calculation. The entire population of the Boneyard Alliance was probably around five hundred men, women, children and Terror Birds. In her opinion, this group through simple attrition could defeat them.

Eva could not allow defeat. Almost on cue fifty mounted warrior pairs from the Rockpile Village arrived. They brought the full assemblage of weapons: spears with spear levers, bows and arrows, slings, obsidian knives, stone hatchets, sacks of pitch and torches. The combined Clans could use young saplings when available and use them to create crude catapults to launch pitch that was on fire. Though the airborne fire balls were very inaccurate, they proved to be a fantastic psychological weapon. Fire raining down from above was devastating. Most adversaries were very terrified by such things especially in the dawn hours. The Clans had improved other weapons as well. Eva had perfected the slings by using hardened clay sling stones. These were all the same weight and size, making them several times more accurate than ever before. A sling expert could kill a man at one hundred and fifty yards with one stone if he struck the person in the head. Her best sling users could hit an animal on the run three out of four times with deadly results.

What to do? She did not want to meet the enemy in the water because the river bottom here was full of silt and mud. The attackers could become bogged down and be at a tactical disadvantage. Eva decided to take half of her riders (twenty-five in total) and rush to the river's edge as a show of force in front of the invaders. She hoped the newcomers seeing the Terror Birds with human riders would spook them. At this point the canoes split into two groups. One headed down river and the other continued forward. Raven gave a warning scream with the familiar three yells each one louder than the one before. Eva ordered the remaining riders to follow the attack boats going down river. Eva took her sling and launched a stone at the forward canoe. It hit the water and splashed the occupants. The response was predictable. Several spears were launched at her position from the lead craft. None of the spears found their mark but the attackers obviously tried to injure or kill anyone on the shore. As this confrontation was happening, another wave of canoes appeared on the opposite bank and were being launched into the river.

Eva knew her sudden show of force, Terror Birds and all, was not enough to discourage a bloody fight. So be it. She had not survived this long to allow her home to be ravaged by these creatures. However, she did wait to see what the first invaders to land on her soil would do. She allowed the initial canoe to land. As they jumped on the shore . . . she and Raven stood within weapons' distance from them. Eva had her warriors stand down their weapons. She stood as high on Raven's back as possible and yelled pointing with her extended hand toward the opposite shore. Her intent was obvious, return or die. The response was a fanatical yell as the group rushed them with ax and spear. The first five from the primitive crafts didn't take ten steps before they were all dead. The next canoe landing did the same thing. Then Eva gave the order to rain arrows, spears and sling stones on the remaining invaders in the river. In seconds half the canoes were denuded of warriors and the remaining turned back and disrupted the wave behind them. Eva was told the white water down river had wrecked the other half of the raiding party. And all but a few invaders that did not drown swam to their side of the river.

The first confrontation ended without one Boneyard casualty. The invaders probably lost thirty members and several more injured. Eva hoped this was enough to discourage this despicable group of humans. It always amazed her how caring, and wonderful her species could be and how awful they could become. What was the difference? She could only speculate.

The Boneyard security force remained camped opposite the invaders along the river. Eva watched to see if she could learn more about these fanatical and violent humans. Each evening they started their ceremonies beating their drums deep into the night. The next morning one or more persons would be hanging from a tree for all to see. Eva prayed the animals would soon tire and leave. However, it seemed more were collecting on the opposing shore with every night of the standoff.

Eva was amazed at their illogical and aberrant behavior. Once something got into their heads, they were unable to turn from its insanity. They shaved their heads, painted their bodies, yelled continually, and beat drums. Those was their good points. At night they would yell louder, beat more drums, and left dead bodies in the trees. At least they didn't kill their dogs to her knowledge. From what she observed the men seemed to be the only members allowed to be warriors, she never saw women or children, except in large groups at the far end of their encampment. A few children were seen but never without an adult female close by and several armed men within eyesight. Her intuition was these women and children were the property of a few war lords or strong men. The rest of the Fanatics were warriors to be expended as the strong men determined.

In response to the enemy's build up, Eva requested more warriors as well. Her contingent grew from the original fifty to a force of well over one hundred and thirty mounted pairs. She dared not recruit more and leave the Boneyard helpless. One of her scouts had reported seeing a group of, what they were now calling, the Fanatics at a part of the river which was above a deep gorge but where the river shores were the narrowest. There were very tall trees on the Fanatics' side. If perfectly cut to fall across the river, the trees were tall enough to form a bridge and allow an invasion.

While Eva was in deep thought, Credo arrived unexpectedly and was very agitated. Eva, Raven and Limp immediately followed. She left her forces under the command of one of her trusted clansmen and took twenty riders with her. Without knowing anything else, Eva sensed what had happened. While her forces had been tied down at the river crossing, the Fanatics had out flanked them in a location she had not anticipated. Credo led them up to the head waters of the raging river. High in the stone mountains where the glacier hung over the ledges like a white and blue giant, Eva could see a line of men negotiating the switch backs that occasionally allowed a direct line of sight. It appeared to her that there were probably at least one hundred armed Fanatics. The problem was they were above her forces, giving the enemy the high ground and a natural tactical advantage. Her heart was in her throat! She immediately sent one of her riders to the river to get reinforcements.

Eva knew she had to stop this flanking force but knew that her remaining troops would most likely be under attack simultaneously at the river and gorge. She had to devise a strategy to delay or defeat the attackers bearing down on her. Hoping the invaders had not seen her war party yet, Eva ordered everyone to remain still and under cover as much as possible. She still might have the element of surprise; however, she assumed when the fight was engaged, she would have no more warriors than she did at this moment.

In these tight spaces she aligned her fighters in the following way. There was a pinch point near a raging waterfall where tall trees hung over a whitewater stream that had to be crossed by the Fanatics. This would cause them to bunch up on the high side of the trail. Her best archers would dismount and climb the tall trees giving them direct shots at the invaders. Any not killed by a hail of arrows and sling stones would be met by the Terror Birds as the enemy emerged from the raging stream and climbed a steep bank to continue their assault.

Back at the river the drums were beating at a frenzy and the ram's horn sounded. The canoes were about to launch and at the gorge the trees were being cut. This time the Boneyard was more prepared. The catapults were ready. On the local Commander's order everything launched. The burning pitch bags flew into the sky and reached the canoes lined up on the opposing riverbank. The fire spread immediately sticking on everything it hit. Many of the assembled Fanatics caught fire and jumped into the water. Some of the canoes that launched overturned. At the gorge the men cutting the trees were within easy range of the archers. Every time one of them took a hatchet to a tree, an arrow either hit the tree or the person with an ax. The boats that reached the Boneyard's side of the river didn't have a chance. Most of the invaders were killed before they got out of their crude watercraft. The Fanatics had upped their tactics and launched rafts up stream as far as they could, and the stable platform of the rafts allowed them to launch their spears with better effect. While this was a surprise, the warriors with the catapults and pitch bags adjusted to assault the rafts. In short order these new war ships were on fire. Within an hour it was over. The assault had been repelled. Again, the Fanatics lost dozens if not hundreds of their warriors. The Boneyard Alliance had some badly injured, but none killed. Eva's messenger arrived long after the assault was over.

The Commander at the riverbank, immediately sent fifty riders upriver to reinforce Raven and Eva's stand. However, it would be at least two hours before they would arrive.

Eva, Raven and their warriors were set. The Fanatics were bearing down on them. She expected to see the first invader to appear above the waterfall any second. She decided to allow the first dozen through without assault. This tactic would bunch the first group of Fanatics together as they tried to climb the steep streambank. The surprise attack of the Terror Birds would then be even more effective. The top of the bank was not visible from the falls. Credo climbed the rocks above the attackers, knowing the sight of a large saber cat would disrupt the already disoriented and frightened attackers once things got started.

To Eva's surprise she spotted what appeared to be some dry brush and dead trees that were piled up just below the trail. To get a flaming arrow there, would be difficult but it was worth a try. She asked for a volunteer to climb a difficult set of rocks to see if she could get a couple of flaming projectiles to ignite the combustibles below. The warrior was to launch her arrows after the first group's weapons were launched at the invaders over the falls. If the fire got large enough this could divide the Fanatics into three distinct sections. The first grouping was from the falls to the steep stream bank, the next from the falls to the fire, and the third section from the fire to the trailing invaders. Credo could then harass the trailing Fanatics, the fire could terrorize the second group along with the archers at the fall's pinch point and the Terror Birds will mop up the most forward group at the steep stream bank.

Once everyone was in place, the Boneyard Clans didn't have to wait long. The Fanatics topped the Falls and were proceeding down the incredibly steep trail. If one lost his footing severe injury or death would likely occur. Eva patiently counted as the first dozen climbed down. As number twelve started to descend, Eva gave the order to fire at the enemy bunched at the top of the falls. Raven gave his familiar war yell and the Terror Birds positioned themselves in anticipation of the invaders reaching the top of the stream bed. The fire arrow flew into the pile of brush, tree limbs and dried tree trunks.

Eva thought she didn't have enough arrows, sling stones, and spears to stop the assault but could delay the invasion significantly. She prayed reinforcements would arrive before they were overrun. Eva knew she had cheated death many times in her short life, but this time death might find her. The first arrows found their mark killing at least five Fanatics at the top of the falls. This temporarily halted the descent of the main force. The dozen in the stream bed reached the top of the steep incline. As each one rose above the top, they were decapitated by the large hatchet-like beaks of the Terror Birds. None of the first group were aware of the greeting at the top. However, their headless bodies on the bank would warn the ones that would follow. Behind the falls and between it and the smoke and fire, panic was raging. A few of the invaders fell to their death on the rugged rocks below. Their leaders were yelling and striking their fellow Fanatics. They were pushing some of them off the trail to their death to remind the others to do as they were told. More and more attackers were climbing down the trail at the falls. They even lowered ropes secured at the top to send greater numbers down at one time. As these stormed the streambank, they were being killed by the Terror Birds. However, the Birds were getting very fatigued and it would not be long before they would be overwhelmed. The Boneyard archers were out of arrows and were relying on slings only. The sling stone supply would soon end as well. Eva then gave the order for the archers to climb down and the Terror birds to retreat. It was time to live and fight another day. Everyone mounted and retreated. Their speed would prevent them from being caught by the Fanatics, but the Clan members and Terror Birds were exhausted and needed food and rest.

Eva took inventory. All her warriors and Terror birds were well; a few of the Birds had minor injuries from the fight at the stream bed. Credo was still up in the rocks above the falls. Limp was by her side. She estimated they had killed or wounded about one third of the Fanatics in this invasion group. However, she knew the news of their success would be followed by additional waves of invaders.

After an hour run from the falls, the reinforcements met Eva and her defenders. Eva had to decide what to do. She needed to know what the invaders were doing. She decided to send some scouts back to try to determine the situation. Had the invaders stopped to lick their wounds, or had they continued with the objective to attack the river defenders from the rear? They could have divided their forces and sought other objectives. Eva was so tired it was hard to think. She bet there would soon be more Fanatics following the first group. The enemies' spies would now have open access to the entire region. Even though Eva and her comrades were able to pin down the flanking invaders temporarily, it was decided these Fanatics were like ants in an ant hill. There were simply too many and they were without human reason or compassion having no respect for anyone's life including their own peoples.

Eva decided to remove her fighters from the river. They would disappear into the Basin, where there was water and the Clans could stockpile food. In addition, the combined group could man the tops of the canyon walls and defend the only ground level entrance. She thought; *"we will take the young bison we have pinned in the village and raise them for food. We will then burn the village and use the Thermal area in the Boneyard to deploy attack squads to harass the Fanatics. The enemy will not easily track us because of the maze of thermals, pools, and steam. It will be a graveyard for them if they try. We will keep lookouts in the tall trees and maintain observers all day and all night.*

When Eva arrived at the river, she gathered her forces and told them the sad news. They wanted to stand and fight but she told them their families were more important than their pride. The Fanatics had so many fighters they could lose ten to there one and those odds were unacceptable. She did not intend to surrender but told them never to fight on the battlefield that favors your enemy. "We will fight in a way the Terror Birds did when the human Clan first arrived at the Boneyard. Always fight when you have overwhelming strength, make your enemy fight when you want to and not when they choose. We will disappear into our home-ground, we will watch our enemy until we know more about him than he knows about himself. We will win this war if we are patient and resourceful. We are not surrendering; we are fighting in a new direction and with new tactics. Let us now leave this place and build our Nation into an unbeatable force the enemy has never seen before."

The Beast Versus Eva

Short Story 6
By Linda and George B

She slept but without peace. With the two Boneyard Clans bedded down within the safety of the Basin, Eva should not have been so tortured. She, however, kept having terrible visions. A large human male with an evil countenance kept threatening her everywhere she turned. His name was Beast. She knew he was the strong man of the Fanatics.

Beast woke in anger. His scouts had failed again to find the ghost riders that harassed his forces. Once he had defeated the tiny witch at the river riding her Terror Bird, he thought everything would go smoothly. He had never experienced such aggravation before. Each time a lieutenant failed he had him killed and hung in a tree. It was getting hard to find new leaders wanting to advance up the chain of command. If it were not for the lure of a mate as a reward of service, there would be no one to risk the potential consequences of failure. He, like the previous Strong Men, used deprivation, intimidation, fear, and torture to lead a band of desperate people now numbering over five thousand. His spies told him the territory they had just invaded had sufficient game to last them several months. The bison and elk herds had not yet materialized but considering the small population he had encountered and defeated made it likely that overhunting had not occurred, and the resources would be abundant. The food stores of the Beast and his people were now quickly dwindling; he would need to find adequate resources to restock. There was a delicate balance between having enough warriors to defeat all rivals and too many mouths to feed. The normal solution of the Beast was to resort to cannibalism when things got out of balance. He preferred the younger meat himself. In fact, many times he would feast on humans over elk or bison.

Beast decided he would survey his new conquest. He had his throne lifted and carried by his house guard and was off on an excursion. He was wanting to relocate his capital from one side of the river to the new land. His primitive throne was placed on a raft and he was pulled across the river secured by ropes. When on the other side, the guards picked him up again and took him to the locations they had picked out for his review and approval.

Eva, was now awake and was meeting with the night scouts. They reported on the enemies' locations and activities. It seems the Fanatics always sent their spies out as three member teams. Initially, Eva had every team encountered killed on sight. However, she changed her strategy. She wanted to capture a few and confront them personally. The scouts this day had captured a trio and were holding them in the primitive Rockpile dungeon. Raven, Eva, Credo and Limp left immediately for the old village remains.

Before they arrived, the Bird Riders tied the three from a Fanatics' recon team to trees that were close to each other. Eva suspected these spies were doomed by the hands of their own people if they were known to have been captured. All she had to do was to brand them on their shaved heads with the Boneyard's arrowhead symbol (using a heated arrow tip) and they could never return to their people. Instead, if they were smart, would exile themselves to locations unknown to the Beast for the rest of their lives and thus no longer be a problem for Eva's people as well. She dismounted Raven, walked up to each one and looked them in the eyes. In the first two she saw fear and they turned their eyes away and bowed their heads. The last looked straight into her eyes and spit into her face. Eva wiped off his spittle and laughed! She had him branded first. Once branded on his forehead just above his eyes, she had him cut loose. He stood reluctantly for a few seconds and then ran off toward the north. Two of the Clan's best Rider pairs followed the Fanatic released. They were instructed to surveil in a way the runner could not detect. Eva then had the remaining two branded on the top of their heads not on their foreheads. She cut them loose and offered them some roasted elk in one hand and a pouch with water in the other. The dumbfounded Fanatics stared at her and each slowly accepted the food and water.

Eva then gave the two stunned Fanatics back their weapons. She turned her back to them and motioned them to follow her. In their bewilderment they followed like puppies. After walking a few yards, a group of clansmen surrounded them. She took a fur hood handed to her by one of the warriors and placed it over her head. She then took it off and gave it to the first Fanatic. Eva dipped her head and he understood. He pulled the hood over his head. The other Fanatic did the same. They were then led to the Basin.

The defiant runner with the branded forehead ran for hours. He finally collapsed and slept until morning. The Boneyard Riders kept a close eye on him but kept their distance. The next day the runner encountered a three-member recon team from the Fanatics. As he approached them, one of the team started to yell at him. The runner collapsed in exhaustion. He was pushed faced down, beaten and had his hands tied behind him. Two of them then picked him up, put a choke collar around his neck and pulled him with them north. Each time he fell they would kick him and spit on him. This treatment went on for three more days. Finally, the four arrived at an encampment. There were probably several hundred Fanatics there. The Riders remained hidden but knew this was as far as they dare go. They returned to report to the Boneyard.

The branded Fanatic was exhausted and had not been given food since his capture. He was bruised, bleeding and battered. Often, he had difficulty in breathing. He was now tied tightly to a tree and his extremities were numb. He heard a commotion and could raise his head only enough to see poorly through his failing eyes. He saw what looked to be a throne with the Strong Man looking at him. His bonds were cut and he fell with a thump. He hit his knees, elbows and head before being roughly turned on his back. Someone threw water on him and the Fanatic runner choked as he tried to breathe. The Beast got close enough to look at the brand on his forehead and slammed his foot into the man's face. The Strongman yelled, smiled broadly, and said a feast would to be had by all that night. The drums began.

The hooded Fanatics were led to the Basin, once inside, the hoods were removed. The two could not believe what they saw. There were men, women, children, Terror Birds of all ages, dogs and near the lake many young bison grazing. There were shelters, campfires, potters, weavers, tanners and flintknappers. The two were led to Eva's compound and given new skins to wear and shown by Eva herself how to use a sling. They started to sign and exchange words and meanings. Raven and his Queen Jewel stood by closely and monitored the process, always ready to kill the two Fanatics instantly if required.

After the meeting with Eva the two were shown where they could bed down and then allowed to roam around. However, they were being watched by someone constantly. For the next several days the process was repeated. The communication got more and more sophisticated. The Fanatics were sharing much about their culture while learning the Boneyard Clan's way of life. There was no doubt that these two were changing daily with each interaction. Eva learned one of the Fanatic's name was Toby.

The Fanatics moved their Strongman, his household, and their food stores across the river, and they settled into a location he agreed upon. The site was on the shores of a large lake which was a three- and one-half day march from the Boneyard's Basin. The site was visible from high ridges above the lake. The Boneyard Riders could reach it in half a day and were sending spies to the overlook daily. Everything important the Fanatics did was reported to Eva and Raven within twelve hours. The Beast was furious. His warriors had not located anything but singular elks and bison. The herds were nowhere to be found.

Within the Basin a change was underway. Eva had given orders to capture as many Fanatic recon teams as possible. Her new recruits would be on the Boneyard capture teams. The first such mission proved to be the pattern to be repeated. She and Raven went on the first such operation. Six mounted clansmen surrounded three spies. They were confronted by Toby and other ex-Fanatics. It was soon determined that one of the three on each team was always a brainwashed plant that spied on the other two team members. When all were branded and released, the spy of the spies almost always fled back to meet his fate. Within four weeks this process captured and branded enough personnel that these ex-Fanatics worked independently with only partial support from the Riders. Eva urged the new group, which was led by Toby, to raid the Strongmen's assets. It was proposed that one raid would kidnap some of the women and children from the new capital.

Eva's strategic plan was beginning to take shape. The Yard's Riders were keeping the bison and elk herds out of the reach of the Fanatics. Others were capturing or killing many of the enemy's recon teams. So far, the war council had estimated the Fanatics had lost twenty percent of their people . . . about one thousand total. Their food was nonexistent, and they were killing and eating more and more of their weaker members.

It was known most of the women and children were sequestered on the extreme eastern side of the camp. The lake was to the north and high ridges with steep cliffs came down from the south. These ridges and cliffs were closer to the congregated women and children than to the rest of the camp. So, the guards were all on the west side of the area where the women and children were isolated. Their attention was almost exclusively turned toward the camp, not toward the ridges above them or the lake. The riders were always on top of the ridge . . . there was only one way up and one way down over two miles south of the lake. The route was only known by the Yard. Large baskets were made, and ropes built that could lift a basket filled with two adults two hundred feet up the steep cliff. After sundown and after the drums were beating, five ex-Fanatics swam at least a mile to the shore on the extreme eastern end of the camp where the protected compound was found. Once there, they contacted a few women walking alone on the shore. The ex-Fanatics told them of a plan to remove any women and children that wished to leave; however, it would happen when the moon waned to its smallest point. This would be in about seven days. The men left and told them they would return after sundown at that time.

Eva knew this was a very dangerous operation. She did not know if the women would spill the beans and there would be an ambush awaiting the rescuers. Her intuition told her this hair-brain plan could work. The personnel risking their lives would all be ex-Fanatics led by Toby and they were willing to take the risks. Her people were going to start pitch fires on the far side of the settlement. They would be there only briefly, but the fires would burn for hours. If the Fanatics tried to put them out . . . they were more likely to spread than if they left them to burn.

Twenty riders crept as close to the encampment as possible. They fanned out and found saplings and configured them as makeshift catapults. Just after sundown they lit pitch bags and launched them as far as they could into the Fanatic's settlement. About forty burning missiles rained down into the far western edge of the Strongman's Capital. The Riders left immediately, fleeing west. After about thirty minutes there were significant fires burning in the camp. The men swam ashore and organized the women and children, rushing them up to the cliff face. Two baskets were awaiting them. Four women went first. On the top were ten Terror birds and greased tree trunks on the edge of the cliff face. The birds hauled the baskets up and returned them in about five-minute intervals. The group was able to safely rescue all the women and children wanting to leave. The group then organized at the top and left as quickly as possible. The Terror birds carried one woman and his rider or two children and a rider. The number of women evacuated was ten with six children. Eva was ecstatic when she met the group that escaped from the camp. They were brought first to the old village. The next day the escapees using the hoods were escorted to the Basin. Everyone returned safely.

Beast was hysterical. How had this attack occurred, and who allowed the Riders to get close enough to his kingdom to burn a large portion of it? He never knew the women and children went missing and no one dared to tell him. Within the women's compound the word was out, there was a possible way out of their miserable world. It appeared none of the women told anyone. The guards were terrified and knew if they reported the loss, they would be skinned alive and then burned to death.

The swimmers returned to the Beast's camp in a couple of days. The women brought one of the guards and together with the swimmers they organized a plan to evacuate more women and children by rafts; the guards would then escape either on the watercraft or go up the cliffs in the baskets. The Boneyard became ship builders. They used willow trees and filled the cracks with pitch. They used polls and oars fashioned out of the same materials. The best archers would be on the top of the cliffs above the lake to pick off any Fanatics that might alert and chase the rafts using canoes. The guards, who had a few primitive craft, would do the best they could to protect the armada. Each vessel would have two oarsmen and two archers. Some of the women rescued earlier volunteered to man the rafts to calm the escapees. A total of thirty primitive crafts were built.

As fate would have it the night was foggy. Especially near the shore. There would be no torches, so a rope was attached between each of three rafts. There would be ten groups of three vessels each. This time the mission began late into the night. It was raining and relatively cold. No one in the Capital would be outside unless they had to be there. However, just in case a diversion was needed a group of twenty Riders were on the far west side waiting for two flaming arrows to be launched from atop the cliffs. The baskets were ready, and Eva was on top the ridge. She could barely see the flotilla approaching from the north. As the first craft got within one hundred feet of the shore, Eva ordered her people to lower her down the cliff-face. They protested but she demanded.

The Beast was bored and restless. He always had trouble sleeping so he took two of his personal guards and left to visit the family compound. They carried torches and walked about a half mile to the edge of his sleeping kingdom. There was a wooden stockade fence with a guard standing behind a closed gate. It had been several weeks since Beast had come to the compound. The guard seeing the Strongman almost froze with fright. The Beast yelled for the guard to summon the women to the large round hut.

Eva slipped into the back of the hut and stood behind the assembled women. She held her obsidian knife the sharpest weapon known to man even to this day. Two of the ex-Fanatics, one was Toby, were standing just on the outside of the hut pressed against the wall. Things were getting very tense. While this was going on, several of the rafts were filled and were quietly being pushed out into the lake. The children were drugged by the herb tea Eva had provided and asleep as their mothers carried them to the vessels.

Eva watched as the Beast yelled at the assembled women. She didn't want to sacrifice even one of these souls by leaving her. So, she did what she thought best. Eva yelled something nonsense and ran out of the hut. Knowing the guards would chase after her, she exited the structure. The Beast's two personal guards following close behind, had their throats slit by the ex-Fanatics from behind. Without a sound the two men died immediately.

Now the Beast was at her mercy. What a fortunate event. In her wildest dream she never thought this could have happened. She motioned for the two men to put on the clothes of the dead guards and drag her back into the hut. All the while she started to scream and cry. Eva had learned much of the Fanatic language over the weeks and used words she knew were correct. Within seconds the other guards within the compound were alerted and came running to the commotion. Eva and the two ex-Fanatics now knew the Beast was in the hut alone and without protection of his personal guard.

She motioned for all the guards not helping fill the rafts to respond to the altercation she was causing. Eva could not believe her good luck. How was this to end? Could she put an end to this nightmare right here and now? If she killed Beast would other strongmen just step into his shoes? She had to decide and quickly. His people were starving, and the Clan's territory could only feed them for a few weeks. Even if they cooperated fully, many thousands would eventually die from starvation, cannibalism, or violence. Eva could not save everyone, so she had to protect her own first.

She had the two newly attired guards drag her in. As they entered the Beast ordered them to bring her to him. They held her between them and faced the Strongman. He looked at her with anger, disgust, and disdain. He picked up his right hand and drew it back to backhand her. While he did so she drew her knife and thrust it into his left arm. It went into his muscle like soft butter. She pulled it out and with a lightning thrust buried it in his left thy and then just as quickly into his right thy. He fell to the ground whimpering. Toby stuffed a wad of fur into his mouth and the two men tied his arms and legs securely. They left him bleeding in the dirt on the floor of the hut.

After the rest of the women and children had been evacuated, Eva with the remaining guards went to the hut. The Beast was writhing on the floor. Eva bent down and looked him in the eyes and asked him if he knew who she was in his language. He nodded . . . yes. She told him: "I can gut you here and now slowly and with much satisfaction or I can let you live, which do you want?" He pleaded . . . "what do you want?" She said: "I will allow you to live if you take your people and leave this territory never to return again. I will be watching everything you do. I control many of your most trusted people, they work for me. Do you understand." He nodded yes.

"Your women will never return to you. Also, the knife I stabbed you with three times is poisoned. The antidote needs to be taken over a two-week period. I will send enough every day to keep you alive if you do what I tell you to do. One slip or deceit on your part and no antidote. I can tell you the death from this poison is very unpleasant to witness much less experience. Do you understand? Here is the first dose of the antidote." She handed him some bitter herbal roots from her pouch. Its taste was awful, but it was both an antibiotic and a narcotic pain killer. So, in her mind Eva didn't really lie. She was just pushing the truth real hard. She turned and left. After everyone was evacuated Eva returned with the two original guards. She had them cut Beast's bonds and remove the gag from his mouth. They cleaned and dressed his wounds as she directed. She instructed him: "Each day come here by yourself and we will give you enough antidote to stay alive. Stay here until sun rise and then you can call for help." She put up her finger and said, "this is your first test. Don't make it your last."

The three ran from the hut directly to the cliff base and jumped into the baskets and were pulled up the cliff. The sun was rising as the three reached the top of the cliff. Eva could barely see the last raft about to reach the other side of the lake. She mounted Raven and they ran down the ridge line on their way back to the Basin.

When Eva got home, she was so exhausted she collapsed, sleeping uninterrupted for twenty hours. Upon awaking, she met for an urgent update from the Scouts. If things were not already enough, she was told the Mammoth Herders were within a couple of days from returning to the hunting grounds. Eva rolled her eyes and almost cried. Then it hit her like a sling stone. One mammoth equaled over a ton of food on the hoof. What if she arranged for a meeting between the Fanatics and the Mammoth Herders, killing two birds with one stone. The Fanatics could chase and fight the Herders in a running battle for the rest of eternity, leaving her Boneyard alone from now on. Now all she had to do was get them together.

Eva sent her scouts out in mass and asked for updates every twelve hours. Raven carried Eva to the ridges above the Fanatic's camp. She sent Toby to the hut to order Beast to ride the basket to the top of the cliff. The Strongman was very sore, but the narcotic Eva was supplying him worked well enough that he made the trip with minimal pain. When he arrived, Eva stood at the northern most position on the ridge. She pointed northeast beyond the lake. She told Beast there was unlimited food past the lake about a day's journey. He stated: "why should I believe you?" Eva responded: "First, you have no choice if you wish to live. Second, I do not wish your people to die of starvation. And last, I want you to leave and never return. Today you will order your scouts in the direction I told you where the food is. Then you will have your people break camp today and follow your scouts. I expect you to have half of your people moving around the lake by tonight or you will not receive your antidote today. You will remain in your camp tonight and return to the cliff tomorrow morning. Do you understand" He nodded yes and returned to the basket.

Eva, Raven, Credo, Limp and about twenty riders remained on the ridge. They were able to watch as yells and screams were coming from the enormous camp below them. The far western end of the camp was beginning to disintegrate and dissolve into a moving mass of people moving around the lake shore to eventually turn east on the far side. Eva, normally stressed and concerned when dealing with evil, had now calmed down, began to breathe deeper and her heart rate slowed. She slept well that night.

When she woke the next morning, Eva's scouts arrived to brief her on their intelligence. They reported the Mammoth Herders were now within one day of the territory but had stopped moving and were resting in a verdant valley where they could graze for a few days. The recon team shadowing the leading edge of the Fanatics reported slow progress because the people were weak from starvation. It looked now that the encounter between the two groups would take longer than first planned. Eva knew she must supply some food to those who would make first contact with the Mammoth Herders. She decided to have her scouts supply bison meat to those Fanatics who were furthest out in front. This would give them a better chance to successfully confront the Herders.

Eva was told Beast was coming up in the basket. She was going to give him three days of antibiotic and pain killer and give him new instructions. The meeting was tense as usual. He appeared a bit stronger and his eyes were clearer. The tiny woman told the Beast the rest of the camp would join the first half today in their march away from her territory. Eva told him he had three days to reach the location she indicated. Assuring him food would be abundantly available once he got to his objective; however, she did not tell him he would have to fight an enemy and hunt down mammoths to eat. Sending him away, Eva reminded the Beast, if he did not leave today, he would receive no more antidote.

Her scouts had surveyed the Herders and told the war council they had about three hundred members. They estimated two hundred were capable warriors. Thus, even a small percentage of the Fanatics should be able to surround and defeat or run them off. If they were smart; however, they would capture some and use them to manage the mammoths. Eva went to the cliff's edge and saw the dust and commotion below. Beast was on his way. She felt relief for the first time in months.

Eva mounted on Raven rushed to the front of the Fanatic's moving column. She was able to assess the condition of the people she was bypassing. They were rather pitiful. She didn't like what she saw but knew she had to persist in her mission.

The Boneyard scouts had killed some elk and left them for the Fanatics pressing forward. The word got back to the trailing masses and they picked up their pace in the hopes to share in the potential food. When Eva heard the report, she ordered her riders to provide as much game as possible without limiting their surveillance.

On the morning of the third day, Eva summoned Beast to her campfire. He came in riding on his throne. His guards were so weak they could hardly keep him on their shoulders. She had his men fed but did nothing for the Beast. Eva handed him a pouch with two more days of the antibiotic but no narcotic. It was time to take him off his pain meds; experiencing a little discomfort would help his focus. Almost laughing at his situation, Eva thought; *soon he might have to walk.*

She yelled: "At your present speed you will arrive at the required location in a week . . . this is too slow . . . pick up your pace!"

Raven came up to her and sat down. She jumped on his halter and they, with the rest of the riders, left the Beast at the campfire. She yelled back they would meet in two days. Within seconds they were out of sight.

The valley in front of the Riders was several miles long and full of hundreds of mammoths. They were slowly circulating picking out the best places to graze and rest. For the first time Eva saw the camps of the Herders. Looking to be easily assembled and disassembled, their temporary structures were very crude but well-engineered. They had a couple of large drags that no doubt were hitched to a few domesticated mammoth to pull when the herd moved. She remembered her experience with this group many months before. Despite their attempt to kill her, was it fair to lead the Fanatics to clash with this group of humans? She still had time to decide. Her first objective was to get rid of both the Herders and the Fanatics. Everything else was secondary.

It had been two days since she met with Beast. It was now time to give him the last doses of the antibiotic. The plan's purpose was to rid him from her territory and facilitate the Fanatics' confrontation with the Mammoth People. This was the pivotal meeting. If it did not go well, she was prepared to kill him on the spot. She had him come to her on the top of the ridge above the mammoth herd. His men carried him on his throne as far as they could. He had to walk the last mile up to the crest of the steep and narrow ridge.

Beast reached the top of the ridge. He was completely out of breath, his lungs heaving with stress. The altitude was higher than he had ever been in his life. Eva looked at him and smiled at Raven, who shook his head and closed his eyes in recognition. After Beast slowed his breathing and was able to concentrate, Eva pointed down at the valley and asked what he saw. He cleared his throat and coughed several times. Finally, Beast mumbled something incoherent and stumbled backward.

After he steadied himself and came back to the crest with Raven and Eva, he said: "What do you expect me to do with those beasts?"

She responds: "I expect you to man up and get food for your starving people. You have no choice. You either kill and eat or die from weakness and starvation where you stand. Send your warriors out in mass and do what you must do! Toby will tell you what is known about what you see and make recommendations on what to do. The rest is up to you." Eva threw the leather pouch with the last dose of medication toward the Beast and said: "We are now through with you. Do not return to the Boneyard Territory. You will be killed on sight. We spared your life only in the hope you will help your people. Now do your job, become a real leader! Your group is too big to sustain itself. You must divide your people into many smaller bands and send them out to other hunting grounds. Otherwise, you will destroy everything in your path and end by eating only your own flesh." She hopped on Raven and left the crest with her lieutenants.

Eva prayed she did the right thing. Like all the decisions made over the years she weighed the potential outcomes of each. She allowed the Beast to live because he had control of his people and was weak and cowardly. Therefore, Eva could control him. Her intuition told her the Strongman would fold to her strength. So far, she was right. What she didn't know was if he could deal with the Mammoth Herders. Could he make the hard choices needed for his people to survive and thrive? Would he attack without warning or try to negotiate some type of trade with their Clan? It will be interesting to see the outcome. She had her scouts keep a close watch on his activities.

Eva ordered her warriors to retrieve the skulls of the Giants from the thermals. She wanted a skull placed at every pass and major access point into the Boneyard hunting grounds. They were told to leave an arrow or spear imbedded in each skull. This she hoped would be a visual deterrent to any future invasions and would forever name their hunting grounds the Boneyard.

The Future Visits the Boneyard

Short Story 7
By George and Linda B

Captain Mona Ann Lisa looks mystically over the thermals, a location that will be called the Yellowstone National Park thirty thousand years hence. Mona is not just the run of the mill ship's pilot and her visit here has profound implications. This place is the epicenter of an ancestor's life struggle. In fact, genetic studies indicate the person in question is the mother of all humans that now exist in the Captain's universe. Her name was Eva and Eva called this unique geography the Boneyard.

This human being started Mona's ancestral line (confirmed by maternal mitochondrial DNA mutation regression analysis) because (Eva's) memories represent the first M-bundles (Memory Node Clusters confirmed by electron microscopic techniques) in Captain Lisa's coded storage embedded in her DNA. Stored memories of Eva (within Mona's genetic memory) were unlocked and found and were estimated to be seventy-five thousand years older than Mona's. While Eva was obviously not the first sentient human, the lack of previous memory in Mona and other humans was theorized to indicate some type of catastrophic event or technical disruption of the code passed down to Eva from her maternal ancestry. This anomaly alone could take forever to research.

The Captain's voluntary memory regression analysis revealed a fascinating story. Eva was a rare individual by anyone's standard. Her story read like a novel and was exceptional entertainment. This woman was simply amazing. Even if one did not allow for the primitive conditions under which she struggled, Eva thrived in unimaginable conditions and was arguably one out of a billion or one out of a trillion beings. Captain Lisa was profoundly drawn to her and felt Eva's story had to be fully researched and shared with creation. So, for her vacation Mona was going to deep dive into the origin of all of humanity's ancestors.

Why is this important? It seems Captain Lisa is the single most powerful entity in several galaxies. She is human but more importantly is the uncontested science administrator and military commander of trillions upon trillions of sentient beings within the major and minor galaxies comprising the Milky Way and Andromeda Quadrant. She like her ancestor Eva fell into her role. Mona did not seek her power and it seems neither did Eva. Mona as Eva thought was simply lucky to have reached adulthood. Both child prodigies were benefactors to their people. Their wisdom, courage and intuition saved the day many, many times. In both cases their parents were pivotal in their lives and created the foundation for their later successes. Both were tormented by dreams and visions that disturbed and just as likely enlightened them.

Mona came here to connect to Eva. You see Mona had the ability to travel in time or at least view history first-hand. It was feared disaster might result if the past was changed; however, science was not certain one could alter the past in any way that would create a new future. Yet, one could return to the past and observe what happened and ascertain how it most likely led to the present. One could study these things forever and Mona did not have the luxury to do so. However, with the resources she had, she wanted to do as much investigation as her time allowed.

Mona came personally to the Boneyard in Mona's present timeline (though 75,000 years after Eva lived there) to get a feel for what her ancestor might have felt. Based on the Captain's geophysics experts very little had changed since her ancestor walked these same grounds. There were thermals that dotted the area belching steam and sulfuric odors continually. Herds of bison, elk and occasionally mammoths visited the immediate area. The Terror Birds that once lived here cooperatively with Eva had long since become extinct; however, they were still found in the southern continent in this hemisphere of Earth. Mona's mind wandered to the global war that had occurred two thousand years ago. It destroyed most surface animals and almost eliminated humans from existence. She herself had just left weeks before five hundred million people had been vaporized, burned, and starved. The ravages of this war were now a distant memory and Earth's population had grown to a few million humans again. Mona returned occasionally to see a fledgling primitive culture slowly progressing from near destruction two thousand years prior but still within Mona's lifespan.

Eva and her people were remnants of the humans that survived the catastrophe that destroyed the high human civilization over seventy thousand years before Captain Lisa was born. The irony was in the same cycle of events that destroyed Eva's world was also repeated in Mona's present time. The difference was Captain Lisa was fortunate enough to lead a remnant from the Earth with their advanced technical culture intact. In contrast Eva was unable to benefit from a surviving technology in her era.

When Mona recounted the decoded memories of her beloved Eva, she felt a deep connection and could almost recite Eva's thoughts without reading them. Thankful to be alive, Eva thought: *I raged against* the *odds, but I prevailed for some purpose.* Mona had felt exactly as her ancestor had thought and visualized. The Captain wanted to know more details than what had been decoded from her DNA. The simple fact was, the only way to discover more details about Eva's life was to observe her ancestor real time, and Mona resolved to do just that!

Captain Mona Ann Lisa returned to her ship the Dragonfly and reported to her Sisters' laboratory quiet room to undergo a process referred to as the Shadowland journey. In this status one could dilate time and go anywhere one had the 4D coordinates for. She had three of the four coordinates by identifying the location. What she needed now was to pinpoint the exact time coordinate to begin her study. This was no easy task. Though certain clues were apparent based on geological and astronomical markers, the precise timing of events thousands of years in the past was most problematic.

In one of the M-bundle dumps was noted a visible comet seen while a total solar eclipse occurred. This was the key to a time anchor from which she could investigate days before and after. This had happened only three times in the last one hundred thousand years in and around the Boneyard.

As she laid down on the padded recliner and started the preliminary pre-launch procedure her heart began to race. Moonbeam her sister placed the headphones over her ears and smiled and gave her a thumbs up signal. Within seconds she lost consciousness and arrived at the predetermined coordinates at the Boneyard. Her body remained on board the enormous Dragonfly Mothership. This ship was the size of a small planet and sported a crew of millions of sentient beings, not all of which were humans. The adventures she had participated in over the past two thousand plus years since her birth were amazing but this journey to the ancient past was equal to anything she had done before. Mona had stared death in the face many times but for some reason this was just as frightening. What would she find? Were there to be discoveries made in her journey to the past that would have implications to her present life and future?

Suddenly sunlight burst upon the good Captain's face and she could sense a breeze. Though her body was not on the Earth's surface her shadowland avatar was. Additionally, her technology was able to simulate the physical senses she would have experienced if her physical body was there. Mona was hopeful her sisters Moonbeam and Levie had, through a process of elimination, chosen the correct time target of the three options. She was impervious to any physical threat she encountered. She had the capability to remain cloaked (invisible) or uncloaked (visible) to anyone near her shadowland presence. Her duty was to remain undetected. The Federation Time Travel Management Council had several guidelines that Captain Lisa must adhere to in her investigation, this one was the most basic. No one time traveling could visibly or auditorily without pre-approval of the Council reveal their presence. Since Captain Lisa was the enforcement agency for such issues, she was not going to defy the guidance.

In her present status Mona was not confined or limited to her human physical capabilities. Simply stated the captain could instantly go where she imagined or wished to be if she kept track of the 4D coordinates of her resting physical body. This technology had long since been perfected and she hardly thought about it.

Not seeing anyone or any living creature at the edge of the Boneyard, Mona flew to three thousand feet above to get a better perspective of the area. Instantly she was there and discovered smoke from campfires in the direction of a large rock ridge. Mona sensed this was Eva's Clan's encampment. She was giddy with excitement as she slowly approached the site, taking in every detail she could observe on her approach. A cloaked physical recording device mounted on a drone appeared and allowed her sisters to observe what their sibling was now seeing. This physical drone was not an avatar. It was real and had been sent back in time as a physical object. This was costly technology and took significant energy and resources to deploy.

There were several clansmen leaving the camp obviously on a hunting excursion. Mona counted a total of six adults, one of the group was carrying a small young person on their back. This tiny package had to be Eva. This was amazing! Mona's first shadowland mission hit paydirt. This normally did not happen. These types of investigations usually took teams of investigators weeks to get this type of result.

Mona continued to observe enthralled and obsessed with every detail. What an opportunity and responsibility. These were precious lives, the foundation of the future, the initial building blocks for thousands of generations to come.

From the manuscript of Eva's memories Captain Lisa knew the Tribe took the young girl on hunting parties because she was the best tracker in the Clan. The child could anticipate danger and steered the warriors into the best location to kill game. Eva's bond with the Clan was exceptional and she was treated as an adult. Though crippled, having been born with a clubbed foot, she became integrated into the survival of her people by the age of seven. Her parents were the healers and midwife of the Tribe. The three of them were highly respected and loved by everyone except for the Clan leader or Chief who saw them as a threat to his power and control.

Mona knew the Chief was to die from injuries sustained in a hunting accident within seven years from this point in time and in an unexpected turn of events Eva would be appointed Clan Leader. Within two years from today Eva's father would find Credo. This young Saber Cat would become the growing child's constant companion and protector.

Mona was ecstatic over her good fortune to establish the anchor point from which further research could be planned. She returned to the quiet lab on the Dragonfly and regained consciousness. Her sisters were already reviewing the sensory data from the surveillance drone. They were laughing and making noises like two teenagers talking about their first kiss. Levie and Moonbeam, were respected as being the best scientists in two galaxies. However, they were acting more like children than serious adults with an important mission to complete.

The three sisters spent hours reviewing the data and the two scientists interrogated Mona until she was so fatigued, she had to leave to unwind. They were already planning a new mission when the Captain left to retreat to her wardroom.

Like Eva, Mona sometimes had disturbing dreams and visions about future events. However, she had not had such an experience for years and years. This was about to change. When Mona entered her suite, she fell to her knees. The flash of light in her visual cortex was overwhelming. It was extremely painful and disorienting. She smelled a pungent odor that was very unpleasant. Mona witnessed a vision, a disturbing sight. Was it a metaphor or a reality? What this meant exactly, she did not know, but never-the-less knew it was about Eva. Situations like this had happened before. There was serendipity in the Captain's life. Mona's fate often intersected or collided with enormous events that changed history. Was this just one more such event? She went immediately back to the laboratory to talk to Moonbeam and Levie.

After she related her vision with her sisters the discussion went on for hours. Seems the Clan leader plotted with his son to rid himself of Eva. What could be done, and should they interfere? They decided to take it to the Time Travel Management Council. From the vision the attempt to kill Eva was a few weeks from the anchor date presently established by their research. Interference by future timelines had been authorized before, however, it was rare and extremely limited. Not until all unintended outcomes were fully investigated and plotted was approval ever granted. Analysis of thousands of outcome deci-sion branches indicated no harm would occur if Eva survived. However, her death prior to her birthing a child provided outcomes that were universally disastrous. The Council with minimal debate approved mitigation with strict oversight. The sisters were required to submit multiple proposals for review and approval. However, Mona was authorized to make necessary emergency modifications if circumstances required. The science of Time Travel had established some mandates of nature that seemed consistent. One such law was interference from a different timeline was a one-time attempt. If it worked it worked, if it failed it failed. Only one chance was allowed. Any additional attempt was blocked by some natural force preventing anyone from returning to that point in time. Because of this restriction Mona was ter-rified. She had one chance to protect Eva, if Mona failed, she and everything she knew and loved might disappear from existence.

Because of what was at stake Mona decided she would physically return to the timeline in question. This was an extreme measure and was reserved only for the most serious situations. She would be by herself and would have the assistance of minimal advanced technologies. Most hardware could not be sent because of its inability to withstand time dilation. However, observation drones were specifically designed and available. Via the drones Mona would have restricted communication with her sisters in real time. She could not travel in her clothing from her era and had to transfer naked. This was incon-venient to say the least. Her normal energy weapons were useless because they would be drained of all power via the transfer and were nonfunctional. This did not leave her defenseless, Mona was an expert with sword and bow and arrow. The problem was both these weapons were not yet available in Eva's era. So, by the rules imposed she had to use those available to persons in the time targeted.

Mona immediately went to her weapons experts and started to practice with a sling and spear. The Captain was a natural athlete having won the equivalent of a Gold Medal in the Olympics as the young-est archer in competition history. Mona found the sling as Eva had, her natural weapon of choice. It was amazingly effective. She could see how lethal it was within a radius of 150 yards. The time traveler spent hours with the weapons and became as efficient as possible within the few weeks she had before the event was to happen.

Based on details in Mona's vision the sisters had determined with 98 percent certainty the day of the event. (They pinpointed the time from the phase of the moon and location of Venus observed by the

Captain in her visual experience) Extreme care needed to be taken as they were approaching the possible event. The Federation could visit only once in any time sequence. So, impatience and premature intervention could lead to disaster at worst and lost opportunities at the least. The Galactic Federation might be the most powerful entity in their era but was almost powerless in the historical crisis in Eva's world. The plan was to send Captain Lisa back to a time three days before the suspected attempt on Eva's life. She was to shadow the Clan and act decisively to prevent Eva's death or injury. This would be very difficult because of the natural abilities and finely honed observation capabilities of the Tribe. The Captain had an enormous challenge. Their plan was to observe undetected until Mona would act. Sounded nice but its execution was a different story.

The day of Mona's insertion began. She had a small pouch with flint to make a fire, a prefabricated sling, spear, stone hatchet, and an obsidian blade mounted securely into a wooden handle. This was the extent of her companions. From these she would have to fashion her clothes, find food and survive until she could act to save Eva. The weather around the Boneyard was unpredictable. At night the temperatures could plunge into the high 30 degrees Fahrenheit and often rose into the low nineties during the day. Without proper protection, hypothermia was a real possibility during the night, especially when it would sleet, snow or rain as was common. A fire at night was required to survive and this would easily lead to detection.

Mona had a plan, but it was distasteful. She would raid the funeral platforms where the Clan left their dead. There would be clothes left on the skeletal remains of the deceased. Over the several centuries of her life Mona had experienced many things most people had never even thought of; however, this was the most disgusting thing she had ever voluntarily done. The graveyard would be the location of insertion, it was separated from the Tribe's encampment far enough to allow the Captain to get established on her mission but not so far as to delay her initial snooping.

Once transmitted to the initial landing site any time traveler would be on their own for several days. To be retrieved too soon after placement could result in irreparable DNA damage and many times death. While the Federation had universal translators Mona would not be able to bring one with her. So, she dove into a crash course on Eva's language. The Sisters had insisted on all communication between Mona and them to be in this dialect for weeks before the mission. This was difficult but the good Captain was a fast study. While not yet conversant, she could, along with sign language, get her meaning across consistently.

It was now time for the transfer. Mona stripped and entered the round capsule with her meager belongings. The Captain nodded and the technicians started the countdown. There was a high-pitched whine and tunnel of sorts opened below her. Mona fell downward for what seemed to be five minutes. Suddenly, she was laying on the cold ground. The landing area was full of low bush cranberry shrubs and one was sticking her in the small of her back. Rather uncomfortable but no permanent damage. The air was chilled, and she shivered. In the small trees around her were platforms where a few remains of Eva's people were decomposed. All that was left were clothes and bones. Mona had her choice. She spotted one corpse looking to be around her size. The nude traveler either got most of her items from one body or selected from several like a buffet. Both strategies seemed disrespectful; however, Mona apologized profusely as if the dead individuals were aware as she took items to cover her freezing body. Surprisingly, the Captain was frustrated because she didn't have a mirror to see how her selections were shaping up. The reluctant thief turned where she thought one of the drones might be and displayed her selections as if she was a runway model. The Sisters were watching everything and between themselves complemented Mona on her selections. While they could see and hear, their wayward sister could not receive sound communication from them. The gawking sisters did however decloak one drone for seconds and sent two tiny light flashes which meant agreement. Mona just used her hand (breaking her wrist) to give the "Oh you don't say" sign.

The clothes selection process took about forty minutes. The thief even found a good pair of leather boot-like foot ware. Moonbeam declared she loved the boots Mona selected and told Levie she wanted a pair just like Mona's. Within an hour the good Captain looked like a native and could feel her body temperature returning to a comfortable range. Finding some leather pouches, she used them to carry the few items brought with her and as a bonus discovered a small cache of pre-selected sling stones. Mona also found two useable slings. She reverently thanked these ancestors and prayed the appropriation of their last worldly possessions would help secure the future for everyone.

Mona had a fantastic sense of direction and had a map emblazoned on her brain. She knew the Boneyard vicinity as well as she knew her own spaceship. The Captain decided to approach the camp to see if she could get close enough to hear or observe without detection. This turned out to be a poor decision. The intruder from the future was not a primitive hunter nor was she accustomed to tracking or sneaking up on game. Eva's Tribe was not as clumsy or noisy as she and quickly became aware of her approach and surrounded the spy within three hundred yards of her objective. Standing with her spear Mona dropped it at the first challenge she received. The petty thief prayed the clansmen did not recognize the clothing she had stolen from their deceased loved ones.

Two warriors came up from behind her and pushed her toward the camp. Mona's heart was racing, and her brain was going a thousand miles a second. Panic was not usually in the highly trained Captain's tool kit. But this time she was totally vulnerable and at the mercy of strangers. She was a fish out of water and this group of clansmen sensed it. Fear was painted all over her face. As they entered the camp the captive was directed at the tip of two spears to the common fire pit. There, what appeared to be the entire Clan formed a circle around her. The Clan Leader, the one who was plotting against Eva approached her directly. He stopped within six feet and stared directly into Mona's eyes. He said in his language; "what is your purpose? Where is your people?" There were muted conversations going on all around them.

The felonious spy knew any lie she used would be quickly discovered. So, the captive used the best words she remembered of the Tribe's language and said: "My name is Mona. I come alone from a Tribe far, far away. I came here to speak to Eva. I mean no harm." The Chief looked stunned and the talking grew in volume. The Clan Leader motioned for the two warriors guarding her to take the intruder away to some unknown location.

She was not bound or harmed; this was a good sign. The guards looked more curious than angry, and she just sat waiting for the next thing to happen. After what seemed to be an hour two persons appeared. Mona sensed the couple was Eva's parents. The female of the pair came up to Mona and handed her some elk or bison jerky. She took the offer and proceeded to eat the gift. The taste was pleas-ant. Mona responded with the phrase "A-Key-yeh" hopefully meaning "Thank you." The woman smiled and nodded her head in response. Then Eva's mother pointed at herself and said in her language, "My name is Sunrise, I am the midwife of the Clan. My husband's name is Rain Child and he is the healer of our people. Our daughter is Eva. How do you know of her?" Mona almost cried but steadied herself.

The reluctant guest continued with the truth that she had started earlier. "In my time and place your daughter is known as a great ancestor, her offspring will fill many lands and worlds to come. She is to be a respected leader, warrior and is wise beyond measure." Looking around to see if anyone else could hear, Mona continues; "I came because she is in serious danger, your Chief and his son wish to kill her." Rain Child, confronted the stranger and said: "How can this be, Eva is deformed and will not have children, it is our way?" Mona took a deep breath and responded: "Eva will not marry someone within your Clan but a member of a rival people who are first your people's enemy and she defeats them against impossible odds, his name is Toby." Sunrise looked in amazement and said: "How do you know such things and what do you want?" Looking into the woman's face Mona says: "I come from many cycles into the future, as many cycles as there are trees in this forest. I come from the stars far beyond the sun and moon. I come to keep Eva from death at the hands of your Clan Leader." The parents looked at the stranger in amazement, acknowledging the obvious hatred from the Chief and his son towards Eva.

Mona felt great relief that Eva's parents were believing her story. She told them the attempt would be made during a hunting mission in the next three days. Rain Child and Sunrise took the captive to their shelter and told the guards they would be responsible for her. The guards did not hesitate the offer and left. Mona was about to see Eva and didn't know how to react. The seven-year-old female was almost towheaded, fragile looking and shy. Her parents introduced her to the strange visitor. Mona did not want to stare at the child and frighten her but she was fascinated by the object of her obsession. She wished to give the child a gift and impulsively pulled out one of the extra slings she took from the graveyard. She asked Eva if she knew how to use it. Eva shook her head no. Mona asked if she would like for her to show her. Eva smiled in agreement. The Captain asked Eva's parents if it was ok to instruct their child on the use of the weapon. They both thought it was fine. Neither of them used the sling and would not have instructed their daughter in its use. The married pair were healers and were training Eva in the healing arts. They had concluded despite Eva's unique ability to track game, her future as a warrior or hunter was limited by her club foot

After Eva fell asleep, the three adults discussed the possible strategies they could employ in the next few days to protect the child. The strange visitor revealed despite her small size she was a deadly warrior. She feared no person and had neutralized many several times her size and strength. If necessary, Mona would take care of anyone that would attempt to assault Eva. However, she needed to be always within weapons distance from the potential threat. The question is how this would be accomplished.

The plan was hatched that night. The Captain would state she knew where game could be found based on her journey to the Tribe the last few days. She promised to lead a hunting party to it. That way Mona would be able to stay with the group that Eva was part of. To Mona's surprise the Chief agreed. He had no reason to fear a tiny female from parts unknown and probably thought he could rid himself of Eva and the unwanted visitor simultaneously. However, if he were to succeed on the hunt his status within the Clan would rise even though Eva was a casualty. The party would be the Chief, his son, four other hunters, Eva, and the strange female in the lead. Mona wondered if the other members of the hunting party were part of the conspiracy. Her intuition told her the Chief and his Son were the only plotters. In their arrogance, they felt they needed no one else involved, the fewer the better.

The hunting party gathered just before dawn. Mona's spear, hatchet, knife, and slings had been taken from her and were replaced with a couple of bone weapons that were all but useless. She was told to lead the way and the party formed behind her. Mona's sense of danger was not yet activated. She was calm and behaved like everything was normal which was awkward to say the least.

Here she was with her back turned to a group of total strangers who were all lethal with their weapons except for a seven-year-old child. Could this get any crazier? The Captain did know where game was. Mona had studied their locations and behavior in the days just prior to her insertion. Leading them to the animals was the easy part. How she would react to the assassination attempt was a different thing. Her brain was churning all morning as she led them to a herd of bison near a slow-moving stream just before a waterfall. There was brush in a deep gully near this favorite resting area for the herd. The sound from the waterfall would cover any noise made by the hunters approaching. The small group could therefore get close enough to the bison with their spears and slings to do some considerable damage.

The stranger led them to the gully and motioned them to assume the stalking mode. They crept down the gully toward the river. While she knew the two plotters could act at any moment, Mona felt the triumph of a good hunt was too important to their political strategy and would therefore not sabotage its success. They positioned themselves as the Captain indicated. She was allowed to place Eva on her back as the rest prepared for a simultaneous and coordinated attack. The Chief gave the sign and they all launched themselves together. Within seconds the herd alerted and fled the area. However, before their rampage, three bison were mortally wounded. This was the most success any hunting party had ever had on one trip in anyone's memory. There would be an immediate feast and bison jerky for months to come. One of the hunters left to bring people from the camp to process their kill in place. This left Mona, Eva, three hunters plus the Chief and his Son.

To help clean and butcher the bison the Chief gave Mona back her obsidian knife. This was a great relief to her. This knife contained the sharpest natural blade known to science. In the hands of an expert it was highly effective and lethal. Mona suspected the Clan Leader would have to act before the additional clansmen would return. This, she calculated, would be about three hours from now. Her senses went on super alert. Mona decided to create the opportunity when she decided not when they decided. She removed herself from the bison processing and picked up Eva and left to clean the excess blood from herself in the river just above the falls. This Mona suspected would be too tempting for the plotters not to respond to.

With Eva on her back the Captain proceeded to the river. She sensed someone was following them. She told Eva to trust her and when she stopped, she was going to give her the obsidian knife. The small child was to take the knife and move away from Mona as fast as she was able. She was to go to the head of the falls where no one could get behind her and stay there until Mona came to get her. Eva was to hide the knife but use it if necessary to protect herself. Eva understood and was ready to act.

Mona heard a loud sound behind her. She squatted down and unloaded Eva. The warrior from the future turned to see The Clan Leader and Son standing above her with spears in hand in attack position. The Captain moved her bone weapons, one in each hand and stood in a defensive stance, crouching, awaiting the next move of her potential assailants. A smile came across the Chief's lips and a smirk on his Son's face. Eva was moving off as fast as she could. The Chief's son acted as if he was going after Eva, but the Clan Leader motioned for him to ignore her and concentrate on Mona. That was perfect as far as the Captain was concerned. Mona instinctively reacted to every move the two made. As they approached, her military conditioning prepared her to anticipate one or both attackers to throw or thrust their spears. They were seasoned hunters; she knew even a small error would lead to her painful death. The warrior Captain practiced this situation multiple times with her weapons experts. Well not exactly like this. In her practice sessions Mona had better weapons than she presently did. While her trainers had guessed correctly about the assault weapons held by her attackers, she was otherwise almost unarmed, not a comforting situation at this moment. The Son lunged first. Eva blocked the spear with her left hand and executed a round house kick that found its full force applied to his throat. He fell immediately unable to even scream with pain. The Chief was next. He attempted to lunge, but before he even moved Mona's knee was crushing his nose. He fell with blood gushing from his face. With both men incapacitated, she completely disarmed them. Taking one of their knives she stood over both and talked calmly.

It was like an angry parent purposely instructing two petulant children. "Now that I have your undivided attention, I would like to have a meaningful discussion. Are you paying attention?" She stuck the knife in each man's face cutting them enough to bring a flow of blood. Their eyes showed fear and anger. The Son having recovered from his inability to breathe tried to grab Mona.

She put her knee in his groin and said "One more move like that and you won't be able to have children from this day forward." Mona turned to the father and pointed the knife at his groin as well. "Again, I ask are you paying attention?" They both nodded yes. "Well, excellent. I know you wanted to kill Eva. I came here to prevent your plans from succeeding. You see I am her guardian spirit. You will not harm her. You will protect her from this day forward. If one hair is harmed on her head, I will hold both of you responsible. That means you will die if you are lucky. There are things worse than death. I will be staying for a few more weeks to see things are properly done. However, I will know what you are doing continually." Mona waved her hand and three drones appeared over their heads. The lights were blinking feverishly. The two men on the ground looked up in disbelief. "These are watchers, they never tire, and they never go away. They are invisible except when I command them to appear. If you wish to die now, I will accommodate your wishes, if not, both of you will live at least until Eva grows into a young warrior." The Captain waves her hand and the drones recloak. "Now get up and return to butchering the bison. And I mean now!" They both scrambled to their feet, picked up their spears and ran back to the processing area. Mona just stood there and smiled for a few seconds before she turned to retrieve Eva.

Over the next few weeks Mona instructed Eva on the sling, teaching her how to swim, military tactics and the basics of martial arts. She told her parents that they would find a juvenile saber cat in the years to come. This animal was blind in one eye and needed to be rescued and protected. The animal would become Eva's constant companion and protector. As Mona was a common sight within the camp, the Chief and his Son retreated into the shadows. The day before the Captain was to leave she told Eva and her parents that she had to return to her people and the next morning she was leaving. Eva was very sad but had strengthened remarkably in the few weeks spent with Mona. The Captain sent word that the Chief and his son should meet her outside the camp.

Mona was sad to leave but hugged Eva and her parents. She held back her tears and turned to leave. Eva stopped her and handed her mentor a small gemstone, it was turquoise. Mona accepted it and thanked Eva. She told her it would be one of her most prized possessions. The emotional visitor then left to meet the two reprobates outside the encampment. On seeing the two the Captain almost became sick. She told them she was leaving but would return if they ever attempted to harm Eva or her parents. They both acknowledged her threat before she left.

Captain Lisa with her weapons ran out of the camp and into the trees, she was returning the clothes and items to the Clan's graveyard. Before the return she stripped and placed the items as best she could where she found them. She again apologized for her larceny and thanked the donors for their help. It would be from the cemetery she would return as she arrived . . . naked and cold. But this trip would be with a small turquoise stone.

One last thing. After Captain Lisa returned to her ship, she scheduled one more trip. This one was to a time after Eva was selected Clan Leader and would coincide with her heart wrenching decision to leave her parents behind to care for the sick and injured during the height of the drought. Mona knew Eva never saw her parents again. The Captain was going to intervene and assure they were taken care of. It was the least she could do for the parents for arguably the most important ancient human nexus in all human existence.

Eva Conquers All but Love

Short Story 8
By George and Linda B

The young woman looked down from her favorite place in her empire, to her credit she had not thought of ownership. The sunset was wonderful. She celebrated being alive. The supreme leader had met every challenge, every threat to her existence. Eva was the uncontested ruler of a territory the size of a country. From her position, no one challenged her. Even the Terror Birds succumbed to her leadership. While triumphant her heart ached at what she had lost in her journey to prominence. Though Eva had overcome every challenge, she, never-the-less, was empty and sad.

The peerless leader lost Limp last winter, her dog she appropriated from a band of Mammoth Herders. Credo her Companion Saber Cat from her youth visits only off and on. Raven and Jewel her loyal friends and leaders of the Terror Bird Clan had their own life and Eva was desperately lonely. As the healer and sometimes midwife she was part of most of the families within her world. This was wonderful but was not fulfilling her inner most needs.

She often dreamed of her parents and grieved over their loss. Eva felt her decision to move the Clan while her parents stayed as the healers to care for the sick an injured sealed their fate. She had no choice. To have hesitated in the face of the extended drought would have starved the entire Tribe.

Her Clan, the Rock-pile Clan, the Terror Bird Clan, and the rescued members of the Fanatics now comprise the Boneyard Nation. All tolled they number 1,500 individuals. They control the area which now includes the Yellowstone National Park, Teton Mountain range and adjacent hunting grounds.

Because of her deformity, the Leader is forbidden by her Clan's tradition to marry and have children. While this custom is not shared by all the people groups in the Boneyard; Eva has so far accepted its edict. However, it has become painfully apparent the burden imposed by this practice is harming Eva. She is now in her mid-twenties and in her time, she is the equivalent to a middle age spinster. Unless she acts soon the opportunity to have her own children will forever be lost.

There is a capable warrior she respects. He has been highly effective and trustworthy and is her highest-ranking lieutenant. The bachelor's name is Toby. He was one of the first Fanatics captured and bears the brand on his head from the blazing hot arrowhead she had placed there. He was at her side the night she thrust her knife into the Strongman's body. The handsome warrior could have turned against her many times but has been loyal to a fault. Toby like three hundred of his Tribe stayed in the Boneyard over five cycles ago. The rest returned to their people in their forced exile from Eva's empire.

Since the expulsion of the Fanatics, the Boneyard had not been invaded or even challenged by outsiders. The Clans had domesticated some bison and were even using them as beasts of burden. Their village in the old breeding basin is still their capital but other settlements were now springing up elsewhere.

Eva has had several recent vivid dreams like when she was younger. Occasionally she dreamed of a child named Mona. She wonders whose child this is. Mona is a name not known to her tribe. However, she remembers a mystery woman warrior with that name who visited her when she was just a small child. This woman showed her how to use the sling, taught her to swim and many other things. Occasionally, Mona appeared in Eva's dreams advising her how to build a bow and make arrows, manufacture a spear lever, and use pitch in leather pouches to catapult burning missiles to frighten enemies.

It was time to ride the perimeter of the hunting grounds. Eva normally rode on Raven's back. However, he was getting older and his son Sprinter accompanied her this time. Sprinter was an extremely handsome and large Terror Bird. He was a good foot taller than his father (some ten feet tall) and probably weighed nine hundred pounds. He was enormously strong, fast and had endurance unequaled in his Tribe. If it were not necessary to stay with the rest of her surveillance party Eva could have covered over eighty miles in one day. She had three other riding pairs in her group, Toby being her senior Lieutenant always stayed to her left and slightly behind her, he was riding Sprinter's sister Topaz. One other mount pair stayed in front and one to her trailing rear. To the Boneyard Nation, Eva was precious cargo to be protected at all costs. The team was specifically interested on the health and numbers of elk and bison herds. They checked the fish spawning areas and the waterfowl breeding areas as well. All surveyed looked abundant and healthy.

They camped for the night at Eva's favorite spot. The site had a fantastic scenic view of the wild river whose head waters originated in the mountain glaciers in the center of their wilderness nation. She walked to the edge of a ledge which overlooked the river and stood there as the sun sank below the horizon. The rest of her party was preparing the fire and putting a stew together. They were able to find mushrooms, wild onions, with freshly killed elk. The Terror Birds were feasting on much of the carcass, while the humans selected the most tender portions of the elk for their meal. They used a terracotta pot manufactured for such a purpose. The smell of the cooking meal was mouthwatering. While Eva knew herbs and the healing application of natural plants and minerals, she was not a cook by any measure, this was one reason she loved these trips . . . she could eat other's cooking.

The Clan leader carried with her a round bowl in her pouch along with her manufactured sling stones. This bowl was for a stew and any tea that was brewed. Eva carried another pouch which contained medical supplies including dried leaves and mushrooms that were antibiotics and painkillers. The healer kept strips of leather and select sticks to use as splints and tourniquets, she carried the thinnest gut she could find and a sharp needle for suturing wounds. At the Basin, Eva was training several boys and girls in the healing arts and was proud of their progress. This made her happy and sad at the same time. It reminded her of her parents and brought back the pain of their loss.

Eva had also learned how to heal and treat the injuries and common medical issues of the Terror Birds and bison that now populated her immediate world. It never failed to amaze her that her life was so busy, full, and meaningful but was still so empty. She often cried herself to sleep when alone. This night the supreme leader would have to suppress her normal nighttime ritual and stiffen her spine and conceal her tender feelings. She was the leader, not the led.

In the morning as they broke camp Eva went for a walk to take care of personal business. As she returned there was a very large badger on the trail in front of her. For some reason she had not taken any of her weapons.

This animal was more than Eva's match and she had nowhere to escape nor the speed and agility to avoid being mauled or killed. The animal was aggressively approaching and seemed intent on attacking her despite her desire to avoid a confrontation. Eva thought how utterly ironic. The legendary warrior that defeated the redhaired skunk giants and the Beast, leader of the Fanatics, is dispatched by an angry badger while returning from relieving herself. What an embarrassing story to tell over the campfire in years to come. About the time she was resigned to her fate an arrow hit the charging animal in its chest most likely piercing the heart. The angry animal moved no further. Eva, stunned and speechless, dropped to her knees. When the bewildered warrior recovered her senses, she saw Toby standing over the dead badger.

Instantly, Eva fell in love. In probably the most vulnerable and embarrassing time of her life, the man who had stood by her all these years without her even saying thanks to, just saved her life. The supreme leader laughed hysterically. If she had not laughed, she would have cried. Eva walked over to Toby and whispered very softly: "This is to be our little secret, okay? We wouldn't want everyone to know their leader is an idiot, right?"

He smiled real-big and with a big smirk on his face responded: "Of course I wouldn't want to make a big deal out of the fact I just saved your life. It could have happened to anyone preoccupied with her leadership duties."

Eva slapped him on his chest and said: "If you tell anyone I will, I will, just cry!"

They returned to the team getting ready to continue their rounds. As Toby adjusted Topaz's halter, he winked at Eva. She looked into his eyes and returned a playful grin. What previously was all business started to become a much deeper friendship. When they stopped to allow the Terror Birds drink and rest, they really talked for the first time. She asked him why he stayed in the Boneyard and did not go with the other Fanatics.

He breathed deeply and said: "I saw no future under the Strongman, he was cruel and a fool. The first time I met you, you showed compassion and reason, the decision was easy. You are a natural leader with incredible capabilities and love for your people. Who else could charm Terror Birds to work for her and love it?" Eva, blushed and lowered her eyes. She was obviously embarrassed, not knowing how to take his sincere complement.

The surveying group camped for the second evening. They had not killed any new game, so they all pulled out jerky and some dried fruit and brewed some tea. The Birds only gorged every two to three days when on a mission, so they were satisfied to rest without eating. Eva left the fire and walked off to collect her thoughts, taking her knife and hatchet this time. Toby followed at a distance making sure she was safe but not interfering with her privacy. Eva was very aware he was there and instead of aggravation she was comforted with his presence. She returned to the fire after sundown and settled in for the night. Feelings of warmth and companionship flooded Eva's soul. Her loneliness diminished. The woman warrior slept deeply for the first time in weeks.

In the morning all were up early and, on the way, their progress was excellent, and they agreed at their present pace they would complete their rounds in three more days. By noon they rounded the north side of the enormous lake within their territory. Eva could see the ridge above the old Fanatics' encampment. This was where she learned to trust and appreciate Toby. Without his assistance she might have died the night she took control of the Beast (Strongman of the Fanatics). Eva's mind flashed example after example of Toby's value to her life. Why hadn't she realized this before? She had no explanation.

That night Toby, instead of following Eva at a distance, walked up to her and asked permission to inquire about personal issues. Eva responded immediately, promising to answer any questions he asked.

Toby first hesitated and then asked: "Why have you not married and had a family?"

She stared at him and said incredulously; "Are you not aware of my people's custom? I am deformed and not allowed to marry."

Toby responded, "I know of no such limitation demanded from you because of your deformed foot. My people do not require such extreme measures. You are no longer just the leader of your first people but now lead all here in the Boneyard. All the clansmen love and trust you with their lives. They would not prevent you from a full life. It would be a bad thing to deny the future the benefit of your children. If you don't believe me, ask them."

Eva was stunned. She had not even imagined having a husband or children. She had never allowed such thoughts, she was overwhelmed. She kneeled and cried silently. Toby, stood at arm's length quietly and did not move. He stood guard as she came to grips with her life. Never in her memory had she felt such deep grief and anger simultaneously. Eva's inner child wanted to scream in rage and strike out but knew she had to get control of herself. They stayed there for what seemed to be hours. She finally stood up and dried her eyes. Not wanting the others to see her, the supreme leader realized she allowed Toby to witness something no one, not even her parents had witnessed. Instead of being embarrassed she looked at Toby and asked him for his silence.

He immediately acknowledged her request and said, "Your heart and person are forever safe in my hands, no one will know this moment from my lips."

The scouting party was on their way back to the Basin and everyone was anxious to get home. The rest of the journey was without incident and they arrived at the Basin just before nightfall. As they entered the village, the children rushed to welcome Eva home. She gave hugs all around and acknowledged each child individually. The older adolescents came to find out when she was going to start their instructions again on healing and other arts. Toby was always amazed at Eva's unlimited energy and concentration. She was such a rare and endearing person. His respect and affection grew with every minute he was near her. Here and now Toby decided to gain Eva's hand in marriage.

How was he going to accomplish his objective? What would win the Clan leader's heart and convince her to marry him? He planned it like a military campaign. First, he went to her Elders to out flank any objections she might use to turn him down. Since she did not have parents, they were the next authority in line. As was the Clan's custom, the oldest man and woman would officiate any wedding. The meeting was tense at least from his point of view, he had all his logical arguments to use in his defense. To Toby's surprise they were delighted. They not only supported his campaign, they asked what took him so long? So, he took the opportunity and asked them how to win her heart. Their response was simply, continue what you are doing. The jubilant warrior left walking on air.

Flowers were nice, new buck skins were good, but food was the best persuader. Eva might have a sweet tooth. He decided he would hunt down some bee honey, and pinion nuts to make a confection to present to her. Since she was a self-admitted dunce when it came to cooking his interest in such things might prove to be beneficial to his plans. This was the ammunition he chose to use first.

The nervous warrior showed up at Eva's compound with a basket with his honey creation. She met him outside and asked what was in the basket. He told her if she would take a walk with him, he would show her. The delighted woman acted as if she had to decide and finally relented to his request. They walked down to the lake and sat on a few boulders at the edge. The moon was reflected off the water and the air was chilled.

The frightened Toby stammered with tension, and finally said, "I made these for you." She quickly put her hand in the basket, and he snapped the lid shut. She screamed and quickly removed her hand. Toby, said: "Not so fast, you need to promise me something first."

She protested: "That wasn't very nice, what do you want?"

He responded: "You need to go with me to the Thermals to watch the Thunder Bird pairing ceremony, Sprinter and Topaz are both choosing their life mates."

"Oh, is that all? I was going to ask you to go with me!" Eva said in a coy way.

"Then it is a date." Responded Toby.

"Sure, now let me see what is in the basket" Eva, pleaded.

Eva, Toby, Jewel, and Raven are standing together on the edge of the steam clouds arising from the thermals. There are two groups of four Terror Birds. A total of eight in all looking at each other with a space of about twenty yards between them. The males are closest to Eva and Toby. The females farther away. Jewel and Raven, start to snap their enormous beaks and stomp their feet in an alternating cadence. It is both rhythmic and hypnotic. The females close the distance between the two groups and start to circle the males as they separate with about ten yards between each male. The males stand as tall as they can and become motionless. Then one female comes up to Sprinter and pulls a feather out of her side and places it at his feet. Another female does likewise until there are three feathers at his feet. Only his sister Topaz plucks her feather and leaves it at the feet of another male. Two males receive no feathers. Toby thinks: *Wow, what a disappointment for the two rejects.*

The male with Topaz's feather at his feet is named Runner. Sprinter and Runner pick up one feather each and rush off into the steam clouds. Topaz and a female named Garland immediately follow the males that took their feathers. The remaining two males and two females repeat the same ritual. The rhythmic beats performed by Raven and his mate continue until the choices have been exhausted. One male and one female remain unmatched and the ceremony stops. Three pairs were chosen, and one will be left for the next cycle. The pairings are permanent, only death of one of the mates will result in a repairing ceremony. Toby is exhausted. He was crushed because not all the pairings were made. Eva was delighted that Topaz and Sprinter found their mates.

When they returned to the Basin, Toby was sullen and dejected. Eva had a big smile on her face and was animated. She was joyful and suggested they go for a walk. Though mildly depressed Toby agreed to do anything to spend more time with the object of his efforts. Eva spoke first: "If you were a Terror Bird and no female left a feather at your feet, how would you feel?" Toby responded: "Are you kidding? I would feel like running into the fog and never returning." Eva laughed and her eyes gleamed with mischief. She told Toby to close his eyes and stand very, very still. She then told him to hold out both hands in front of him. Eva took a feather from her hair and placed it in his hand. He felt its near weightless touch on his palm and fingers. He couldn't believe what she did. He was speechless. She whispered: "You can open your eyes now."

Toby, said the only thing in his head: "I may not be a Terror Bird, but I think I know what you just did, right?" Eva nodded and Toby continued: "I don't see any fog bank to run into so, instead, I will just stand here and say, I can think of nothing more I want to do than be your mate for the rest of our lives." He laughed with joy and picked her up in his arms and swung her around until they both fell from dizziness.

The village was buzzing with activity. The common area by the lake was congested with hundreds of people, including dozens of Terror Birds in the back so they didn't block others line of sight. Nearest to the lake stood the two elders of Eva's Clan, the oldest woman and oldest man. In front of them was a hide laying on the ground. From different directions Eva rode in on Raven and Toby rode in on Topaz. They dismounted and the women quickly surrounded Eva and tied her hands behind her back and put a fur hood over her head. The men did likewise to Toby. The two were led to the two Elders and placed just behind the hide. Both stood motionless.

The woman asked first: "What woman asks to be married?"

Eva yelled, "It is I, Eva."

The male Elder asked: "What man asks to be married?"

Toby responds, "It is I, Toby."

The woman said, "Bring these two forward but first cut their hands loose and take their shoes. Let them feel the same ground and bind their hands one to the other."

The attendants cut their bonds and loosely tied Toby's left to Eva's right hand. The Elder male then asked: "Do you freely agree to this oath and do you acknowledge the Creator who protects your union?"

They both answered: "I do!"

The Elder woman ordered the attendants to remove the hoods. Eva felt the hide under her feet and knew the texture was wrong, she looked down and smiled knowingly. They were standing not on a bison or elk hide but on the hide of the badger that almost took her life and brought Toby into her world. The woman told them to look upon their new mate. The badger hide was rolled up and handed to the couple. The old man loudly announced: "This hide is the foundation of your new life. Remember you stand on the same ground from this day forward hand and hand."

The celebration went on for hours, that evening a strange circular light (never seen before) erupted over the lake for several minutes. This was taken as a good omen, the creator acknowledging the new union between Eva and Toby.

Post Script

When Mona returned to her mothership the Dragonfly, she met with her sisters and they went over their findings and compiled a report for the Time Travel Management Council.

She was exhausted from her so called vacation and needed to rest. While in her favorite spot in one of their wilderness biospheres, Mona rolled Eva's tiny turquoise stone repeatedly in her fingers. She decided to confront the Council with a request she felt was ethically proper. At the meeting she pleaded her case. Captain Lisa asked the council to allow one more mission to Ancient Earth admitting she had already taken the liberty to schedule. This mission was to target coordinates ten years forward in time from the mission she just completed that saved Eva from assassination. After considerable debate and assurances that no disruption in the future would result her request was granted.

Mona immediately coordinated with her sisters to plan the excursion. This time most activities would be using primarily the Federation's Shadowland capabilities and only one brief personnel inser-tion. Mona went to the quiet lab and prepared for the journey. Levie put the earphones on Mona and she lost consciousness. For weeks prior, the sisters had been interrogating the memory manuscripts to pinpoint the exact time and location Eva's parents were left in place to take care of the sick and injured. It was assumed Sunrise and Rain Child, never left the locality but succumbed to starvation or injury. It was assumed they died within days or weeks after Eva evacuated the clansmen that could travel to the Boneyard. Mona's first journey to the past would try to confirm the details.

The area observed by the 4D coordinates chosen by Moonbeam and Levie, was desolate. There were the remnants of an encampment near a failing water source. Mona saw only three tent like shelters that were still standing as if tended to. As she went forward, she was getting very depressed sensing the awful things she would be seeing. In one of the tents were three older clansmen, all dead. In the other shelter there was no one to be found. That left the last tent and Mona became frightened of the possibilities. There she found two starving persons, alive but comatose. To her remembrance these were Eva's parents, they were ten years older and mere shadows of themselves. Her assessment was they could not live but a few more hours.

The Captain returned to the laboratory and suddenly awoke. She told the technicians to prepare the time dilation capsule for use immediately. She stripped and jumped into the capsule. Within minutes she was laying on her back in the desolate compound. She rushed into the shelter and moved the couple to within inches of each other, Mona then laid over them and put her arms around both and continued counting down. When she reached one hundred, the trio disappeared from the miserable tent. Within a few minutes, they were on the Dragonfly. A medical team gave Mona a jumpsuit and took the couple to intensive care. The two were placed further into an induced coma and given liquid nutrients and I.V. therapy. It would probably be a few days before an attempt would be made to awake them.

In the meantime, the three sisters and a host of primitive culture experts tried to design a way to decompress and orient the couple to their new surroundings and life. The plan was to take them to a wilderness biosphere and slowly revive them over several days. Since these two were highly observant and intelligent people it was expected they would eventually adjust; however, great care would be taken to integrate them into the highly sophisticated, complex, and technologically advanced future.

After several days Mona was briefed on their progress. As of today, they were to be free of all medication that would suppress their perceptions or curiosity. Mona put on some fabricated hides and primitive gear they had thrown together. She put Eva's gemstone in her pocket to help prove who she was just in case the couple might not recognize her. With great hopes she took a deep breath and went to meet them.

Rain Child and Sunrise were setting at a waterfall and Captain Lisa walked up on the other side of the pool between them. Mona waved and they waved back. Since in real time the Captain had only been away from Ancient Earth about three weeks, she still remembered their words, expressions and language. They had aged ten years since their last encounter with her, but the advanced nutritional and medical technology of the Federation had taken twenty years off them. They looked younger now than they were when Mona left them.

She walked around the pool and approached. When close enough she asked them in their language if they remembered her. They both answered yes. Mona asked if they had questions.

Sunrise, asked: "Just where are we and have we died?"

Mona smiled and answered. "You are both quite alive and you are no longer on the Earth. Do you remember I told you I came from beyond the sun and stars and from many, many cycles that had not happened yet." They both nodded yes. "Well, you both are now in that same place. You have nothing to fear here. You are our honored guests and I want to show you something. Your daughter Eva is okay. However, she has grieved over your loss for many cycles. I am not able to let you talk to her, but I will let you see something wonderful. I am going to show you where she is ten years since the time she left for the Boneyard. The celebration you see is in a basin near the thermals area of the hunting grounds. You will see some amazing things. We can fill you in on the history in the months to come; however, trust me what you see is real."

The hidden drones were showing the wedding ceremony from three different perspectives. Eva's parents were enthralled by every detail. The technology allowed them to hear, see, smell, and even feel the breezes and temperature surrounding the event. Eva's mother recoiled in shock when she saw what looked like her twenty-five-year old Eva ride in on an enormous Terror Bird with a Black Plume on his head. Rain Child reacted simultaneously as well. Mona forgot they had never seen such a sight. These birds had been their most feared competition and predators.

Mona stopped the transmission and explained. "Your daughter was able to create an alliance with the Terror Birds. They are highly intelligent and capable animals; Eva communicates with them, and they are close allies. Raven, the bird she rode in on is their Clan Leader. In fact, Raven, and his Queen Jewel, live within Eva's compound."

The two looked in amazement as Mona turned the transmission back on. They watched the rest of the ceremony and were stunned. Along with Captain Lisa they watched the aftermath of the wedding and the celebration going on into the night. Mona was just as mesmerized as Eva's parents. She cried with the parents multiple times. Eva looked radiant and beautiful and Toby was no ugly duckling either. Before they turned off the drones, Mona said, "We are going to do one last thing. One of these observation drones is at the end of its capabilities. We are going to send it to thirty-seven thousand feet and detonate it in a series of visually brilliant demonstrations of light." Within moments one drone left the surface and within seconds it was looking down on the dark earth below it. As the other drones recorded, there appeared high overhead multiple circles of light, some of the best fireworks anyone could have designed. It took about three minutes for the light show to dissipate. Eva, Toby, and the Boneyard would forever remember the light show and the wedding ceremony.

The Namesake

Short Story 9
By George and Linda B

As a practicing midwife, Eva knew all the telltale signs and symptoms. Her morning nausea and extreme mood swings and emotional storms were all the proof needed. One of her students would now have to nurse her into motherhood. She was older than others who had their first child. She knew the process and dreaded the worst parts of the grind to parenthood.

To complicate the situation, she and Toby (her first and brand-new husband) were the vanguard of the security and governance of the Boneyard. She was not elected, nor had she ever sought her position. Before Toby became her mate, she alone was the undisputed ruler over an enormous wilderness nation which included the entire Yellowstone National Park, the Teton Mountain Range, most of Wyoming, Montana, Idaho and parts of Utah and Colorado.

With Toby and a small army of warriors riding Terror Birds (seven-foot-tall flightless birds), they patrolled their boarders and evaluated the wildlife for signs of stress, disease, or poaching. They had a schedule based on the seasonal shifts in weather and animal behaviors.

Eva surmised she was two months into her gestation. The birth rate among humans one hundred thousand years ago was very low. Women ovulated once each annual cycle not once every full moon phase. Each pregnancy was therefore precious and anticipated with great reverence as a gift. Her's would be anticipated by an entire nation. She was not yet prepared to announce her condition; fearing the demand to forego her trek riding atop Sprinter for hundreds of miles.

The warrior queen wanted this last ride around her beloved Boneyard Nation before motherhood took center stage for several months. She already knew her child was a girl whose name would be Mona. No one in the three tribes of her country had this name. This was a name from her childhood and her dreams. The guardian, Mona, would sometimes come to her in dreams and visions imparting wisdom and useful concepts.

When Eva was seven cycles old, a stranger had appeared one day and had messages for her parents. This woman saved her life and stayed with her people for several weeks. She was an amazing person, wise, resourceful, and kind. Her name was Mona and taught her how to use the sling, how to swim, how to defend herself and to think as a warrior.

This morning was the first day on the trail and Eva was angry and getting more irritated at Toby for not inventorying their supplies properly before their departure. The normally detailed and compulsive Toby had carelessly forgotten to bring her medical supplies. As the senior healer, midwife and surgeon, Eva just knew she would have to improvise if some unexpected injury was to befall the team of fifteen warriors and their mounts. Though still technically newlyweds, this was to be their first old married couple moment.

To Eva's relief, Toby informed her after her emotional reaction, that by the second night a rider would meet them with additional provisions to include her medical kit. Not to worry, he had it under control.

Eva thought she was now going to have to reveal her secret to her husband or she might not make it back from their journey. For years she had warned couples awaiting their first child to expect emotional peaks and valleys, never thinking she would one day fall prey to the same experiences. These travails were not anticipated because she had a club foot and was therefore, not allowed to marry and of course, children were out of the question. This custom of her Clan was to prevent genetic deformities from being passed down to future generations. Only when other traditions were introduced into her burgeoning nation did this custom fade away.

That night Eva decided to tell Toby he was to become a father. How did one do this, especially while in the company of warriors on a mission where privacy was minimal?

Once the company had bedded down for the evening Eva took Toby to her favorite place in the Boneyard to experience the sunset. There they held hands and faced the yellow, gold, and red rays of light. Reluctantly, Eva turned toward Toby . . . but before she could say anything he firmly stated; "Little Badger, you are pregnant, aren't you?"

Eva, sucker punched him in the solar plexus. As Toby was recovering from the force of her assault, Eva smirked and said: "Yes, I am! And you should have waited for me to tell you, you spoiled my surprise!"

Toby interjects: "Trust me I am excited, ecstatic and thankful at the news. I suspected your condition for some time now." In mild aggravation Eva asked: "But you don't know the child's sex or name, do you?" Toby returns volley: "Well, I guess not. Are you going to tell me or keep me in suspense?"

Eva inquired: "Since you know, does everyone else know?

Toby retorted: "Well yes, it is talk of the land, everyone is taking bets on when the child will be born and whether it is a girl or boy?"

Eva raises her voice and demanded: "Why didn't you tell me!"

Toby responded: "I knew you would get around to it when you were ready."

Eva demeans herself: "Good, graces . . . if I am not blind, dumb and stupid!"

Trying to appease Eva, Toby pleaded: "Don't be hard on yourself, you are beloved by all and adored by me, our child is blessed to have an entire nation to care and raise it. So, are you going to tell me more?"

Eva sarcastically responded: "I will have to think about it, maybe I should wait for the whole lot of them to name her!"

Toby immediately celebrates: "So, our child is a girl!"

Eva responded: "Yes, and her name is Mona."

Toby complained: "Mona, what kind of name is that?"

Eva forcefully stated: "It is a great name, a wonderful name, so get use to it!"

Toby pleaded for forgiveness: "Okay, okay… it is sort of catchy, it will grow on me. So, when will she be born?"

Eva responded: "In about seven moon cycles"

The rest of the trip went as expected. The elk and bison herds were thriving. The spawning areas were flush with the proper level of water and the waterfowl were nesting appropriately. Thank goodness the mammoth herds had avoided most of the beaver damming areas this year. There was no evidence of poaching or incursion of other human tribes.

Within thirty days the team returned to their Capital (the old Terror Bird Breeding Basin). Eva was beginning to show, and it was now completely obvious. The official word was announced at the lake-shore communal fire pit. The crowd was very large. Several hundred people and Terror Birds were in attendance.

The oldest man and woman of the Clans along with Raven and Jewel (Clan Leaders of the Birds) stood together and performed the simple customary ceremony. In this celebration a hide worn by Eva was removed by the eldest woman. She handed it to the oldest man, and he spread it on the ground. There the people came by and placed any memento, gift, or craft they wished to give Eva, Toby, and their future child. It became quickly apparent the hide was way too small for all the gifts.

Eva was not into possessions so this custom to help new parents to her became a logistics nightmare. She was already very wealthy in earthly bobbles and did not want to offend anyone's act of kindness. So, she selected one item which she held up for all to see and asked everyone to return to get their offering. All did so without complaint. What she kept was a small but beautiful turquoise stone. It reminded Eva of the stone she prized as a small child, which she had given to Mona, the stranger who taught her so many new things before she left. Eva thought this stone would be given to her child when she was old enough to understand its meaning and attached history.

Eva's pregnancy proceeded normally, and Mona was born a healthy baby with blond hair and blue eyes. Her hair and eye color were the same as her mother's at her birth. Eva's hair turned brunette later in her youth and the same was expected for Mona later as well.

Eva didn't tell anyone that the first time she saw Mona she counted each of the newborn's fingers and toes twice. Her infant was a perfect little girl. No sign of any deformity. What a relief! Eva's fears were not irrational; she prayed her child would never struggle against the obstacles she had to. Her club foot made her childhood and adult life so different than all those around her. Eva in her most intimate feelings fought each day to overcome her handicap. She was thankful to the Creator her child did not have to suffer as she had.

Though physically perfect, Eva's child was far from normal. Mona was so unique many would call her weird. She seldom cried and refused to speak when other children were already conversing. She preferred sign language and intuitively anticipated everything her parents wanted. It was like she read their thoughts. She spent much of her day around Jewel and Raven. The two elderly Terror Birds and she were inseparable. Eva always knew where Mona was when out of sight. The active child was on Raven or Jewel's back. Toby said Mona was more bird than human.

These behaviors persisted until the bird child was in her early teens. Mona would accompany her parents on their inspection tours. Raven and Jewel would often tag along to babysit and protect the youngster. This gave Toby and Eva great freedom to perform their official duties, so they never considered Eva's preferences as a burden or strange. It never occurred to them their daughter was essentially being raised by two 700-pound flightless apex predators.

One day Mona spoke clearly and with great authority. To everyone's amazement she announced there was an enormous threat to the Boneyard. Eva was stunned. Ecstatic over Mona's newfound verbal skills but disturbed over her proclamation. Eva did not know whether to cry or laugh. So, she did both. Toby followed suit.

The young prophet could not give specifics but was certain of the impending dangers ahead. Eva understood her daughter could have such premonitions; she had often had the exact same experiences. However, this was the first time Mona had communicated such feelings.

Temporarily ignoring this enormous threat, Eva felt it was time for a Mother-Daughter talk. She asked Mona to take a private walk with her. Mona complied but was hesitant. Eva thought this was going to be difficult but necessary. As they proceeded to Eva's favorite spot overlooking the whitewater river, a calm came over her. She felt her daughter's turmoil but also sensed a great peace as well. Eva comprehended a deep wisdom and knowing. Her love for her daughter was the strongest feelings she ever experienced, she and Toby would give up their lives for her without a second's hesitation.

Suddenly during their return walk, Eva was jolted with a scene of destruction, fire, steam, heat, and flowing lava. Though a vision, she knew it was real. She was dumbfounded. Her daughter was right. But how much time did they have? They must act, plans must be made, and scouts sent out immediately to evaluate the situation.

After a quick discussion with Toby the three went in opposite directions. Mona went with Raven and Jewel and three riders north; Toby went east, and Eva went west. Another trusted scout went south. They were to meet at the Basin within two weeks.

Mona's vector took her deep into the ancient caldera that formed the bulk of what is now Yellowstone National Park. The thermals, hot springs and geysers were extremely active. The sulfur dioxide was dangerously high and prevented them from penetrating areas normally accessible. Some streams were too hot to sustain the fish and piles of their bodies were forming check dams along the banks and forming shallow pools. They found many elk, bear and wolf carcasses laying untouched by vultures and condors. They felt several ground quakes and aftershocks. They had seen enough. They headed for the Basin immediately.

The four scouting teams met with the settlement representatives as soon as all returned. The meeting was held at Eva's compound. It was a solemn affair. Life had been safe and prosperous since the Fanatics had been expelled over twenty years ago. No one wanted to leave their beautiful and abundant surroundings. This was their home and they loved it. The very thought they would be forced to leave was repugnant.

The teams reported one at a time. No snow remained within 100 miles in every direction, the ground temperatures simply melted everything. Many streams were too hot and polluted to safely drink from them. Game had either died or was being forced to flee at an ever-increasing pace the closer one got to the center of their hunting grounds. The fish, waterfowl and beavers were dead or were too weak or sick to flee and in the process of dying.

The Basin was presently at the outer edge of the most afflicted areas, but conditions were worsening. If things progressed at the same pace as now, it would not be long before things were unlivable. Those present voted to leave. But they had no idea where they could go. All they knew was they could not go north. That would only take them into the heart of the beast. They had no idea how far they must go to escape the conditions they were leaving.

As everyone was waiting for someone to speak, Mona, the thirteen-year-old daughter of Eva and Toby broke the silence. She said in a firm steady voice: "We will follow the main elk and bison herds. They are our food sources, and they will instinctively seek safety and grazing areas. We have 500 mounted warriors; few can stand in our way. The sooner we follow the herds the better. We once were nomads, seeking game and food as the seasons cycled. We will turn to that life until it is safe to return. We now have only a few days left before this ground becomes our graves."

All were stunned by her words and none objected. The die was cast. Mona turned to her mother and said: "You must lead them, without you, most will perish."

Eva, who was stunned, gave the following directions: "Toby, take our best scouts and locate the herds and the direction they are fleeing. Everyone else, we will leave in three days. Make sleds and take warm hides. Weapons are more important than cooking utensils. Jerky and dried fruit is more important than beads. Footwear is more useful than decorative blankets. Do I make myself clear?"

The meeting ended, and all went to prepare for a new life and a new struggle to survive. On the fourth morning the people and Terror Birds were gathered in the common area near the lake. The weather was hot, and the sulfur odor was very strong. Eva gave the last instructions. The lead warriors and their mounts left first. They proceeded in the direction supplied by Toby and his advanced scouts. Within one hour all had left their beloved Basin. No one knew if they would ever return. All were sad and many cried as they cleared the exit to their haven of twenty years.

Many years and thousands of miles later, Eva and Toby were holding a tribal council. The years had been extremely hard, their numbers were half of what they had been when they left their sanctuary. Little Mona, Raven and Jewel left with half of the Boneyard Nation to follow the elk herds. The rest of the Nation stayed with Eva and Toby to follow the bison herds. There had been no meeting between the two division for over nineteen years. Eva grieved for her daughter, wondering if Raven and Jewel were still with Mona. Toby was in good health but slowing down significantly. He preferred to walk instead of riding on Topaz most of the time. Their son Journey was about to turn 18 cycles old. He was just like his father; strong, dependable, and handsome. All the young single women were seeking his attention but so far, he was not showing any favoritism.

Journey was an excellent, tracker, herder, and warrior. He was sure to become a leader at some level and at some time. Like his mother he had a knack for the healing arts, but it was not his focus.

The Bison Clan as they were now calling themselves discovered domesticating bison was not impossible. The bulk of the Clan now limited their seasonal range to within a radius of 100 miles. A far cry of the distances covered just ten years before. Their people now had two settlements, one for late spring and one for late fall.

The young Journey was a quick study, if he was shown something once, he retained it. Little escaped his attention. He saw something that was out of the ordinary and he knew he must talk with his mother. A light was blinking briefly in the sky which was not a star. It was near the horizon. He noticed it for two nights in a row and then it was gone.

When he returned from a scouting trip, he went to greet his parents. After the pleasantries, he mentioned his observations. Eva alerted on the details immediately. She questioned him thoroughly and related an experience from her youth. It seems when she was seven a stranger had appeared and had saved and greatly changed her life. There were brief sightings of strange objects and blinking lights in the sky surrounding some of the events. She wondered if there was a connection.

Mona looked down at the small turquoise stone in her hand. It was given to her by her mother when they parted over nineteen years ago. She was now 32 cycles and was still the leader of her Clan (the Elk Clan). Her husband was the leader of the Mammoth Clan and they had three children. The eldest was a girl, Eve, named in honor of her grandmother Eva. The two youngest were boys named Blaze and Summit.

The stone she rolled in her fingers had been her constant companion and gave her comfort especially in her darkest moments. The years had been difficult. Raven and Jewel had died within days of each other over five years ago. She loved her husband Flint, but they were often apart since they did not share the same leadership roles. Their marriage was originally more of a practical and political alliance than a union based on affection and attraction. They had grown closer over the years yet still not at the depth she desired. Not like her parents. She so yearned to see them once again.

The elk and mammoth herds came within proximity twice each cycle. These encounters with the herds and the Clans lasted for maybe three full moons annually.

Mona was now without her husband and facing a potential crisis. Wildfires caused by lightning strikes had stripped the foraging areas of the elk herds dramatically. They were on the move and her people needed to follow their food source. She had no practical way to notify Flint of her dilemma. So, she ordered the Clan to move and hoped for the best.

Days of hard travel resulted in the death of many clansmen and Terror Birds. Hostile tribes were encountered multiple times in their sojourn. Fighting off raids took their toll. Finally, they ended up in an area one hundred miles from where they started. The location was acceptable and defendable, with sufficient water and alternate food sources. She now had time to rest and reminisce about her life. She had never been this sad.

Eva and Toby were now convinced via Journey's scouting report prairie fires were raging to their south in such intensity and frequency they needed to move their bison herds immediately. So, the order went out to move. This was an enormous risk. They were certain to encounter hostile tribes in their efforts to escape from the fire threat.

So for the first time in years, Eva, Toby and Journey mounted up and headed north with fifteen additional riders to scope out the territory and hostile tribes they might encounter. They rode north for three days without incident. At the end of the third day they saw smoke in the air which looked more like an encampment than the remains of sporadic wildfires. That evening they camped and set up sentries to alert them if attacked.

The next morning Journey mounted up and took two companion riders toward the possible encampment. Within thirty minutes the trio was surrounded by a large war party of mounted terror birds. This was the first time Journey had seen any others like themselves. He had his men throw down their weapons and announced who they were and asked to talk to their Clan Leader. To his surprise they understood his request. The three were brought to the encampment.

Journey was told to dismount and walk into the camp accompanied by two armed guards. He was stopped in front of the central fire pit of the new settlement. Several warriors stood facing him. The men parted and Mona stepped forward to confront the intruder. Mona was immediately struck by this handsome warrior's youth, fearless posture, and strength. She observed him for several moments before she addressed him. She said clearly: "What people do you represent, what is your purpose and what do we call you?"

Journey was mesmerized by the Clan Leader's beauty and authoritative voice. He hesitated but answered. "My name is Journey, my people are the Bison Clan and we seek temporary grazing for our herds." More calmly he said, "We do not seek to fight, we come to share our knowledge and will compensate you for our presence."

Mona, asked: "You ride terror birds as we do, where did you get such knowledge and cooperation from the Bird people?"

The young warrior responded: "It is before my time; however, my parents know our history and will be able to answer any questions you may have."

Mona, quickly questions: "Who are your parents?"

Journey is quiet briefly but finally states: "My parents are the Leaders of the Bison Clan."

Mona looks deeply into the warriors eyes and requests: "What are their names?"

The young man wanting to protect his parents is hesitant but decides to be honest, sensing this woman is not to be toyed with: "Their names are Eva and Toby."

The scouting party was prepared to continue north but was waiting on Journey and his two companions to return. Eva was getting worried about the time the three appeared riding toward them in a deliberate pace. She walked toward them along with Toby. The trio stopped and dismounted. Journey walked to converse with his parents. He reached into his sling stone pouch and retrieved a necklace and handed it to his mother. He said: "The Clan Leader told me to give this to you. The Chief then asked for you, father, and I to return to their camp. The rest of our party is welcome to come later."

Eva eyed the necklace closely and saw the turquoise stone she had given Mona nearly twenty years ago. She was overwhelmed. Eva showed Toby the stone and he immediately recognized the gem. She asked her son: "Describe the Clan Leader to me?"

He said: "I was impressed, she was beautiful, strong and confident, probably in her early mid years, it was clear her clansmen respected her. Also, they were bird riders. They called themselves the Elk Clan."

Eva asked: "Did she give you her name?"

Journey retorted quickly: "No, she did not."

Eva took the necklace and placed it around her neck and said, "let's go."

They arrived at the camp within forty minutes and were escorted by several mounted warriors from Mona's Clan. The three entered the new settlement and dismounted; Sprinter and Topaz accompanied them. The five approached the center fire pit. There the entire Clan was assembled. The proud Elk Clan Chief stood apart from the crowd awaiting them.

Mona restrained her excitement as long as she could. When they were within twenty yards, she ran toward them and jumped into her father's arms. She hugged and assaulted Eva next and later attacked Topaz and Sprinter. Journey was stunned beyond recognition. His parents had not warned him at all. He finally realized this person assaulting his parents was his sister Mona.

After Mona calmed down, she told her long lost parents she had a surprise for them. She turned behind them and motioned. Three young people separated from the onlookers. The first was a female and then two younger male children followed. She presented them. "this one is Eve, the next is Blaze and the last is Summit, these are your grandchildren."

There was a celebration that night as a grand reunion took place. New introductions and new memories were created that would last for lifetimes. After most were exhausted and fell asleep, Eva took Mona aside and they walked together in the moonlight and stars. Eva now sporting more gray hair than brown was awestruck at her daughter's beauty. During the walk Eva returned the necklace with the turquoise stone to Mona.

Eva explained: "The stone in this necklace is to follow your blood line from this day forward, I believe it is magical. When the Boneyard Nation honored your father and I with gifts anticipating your birth, this appeared on the gift hide and was the only offering I chose to keep. It was also the only gift that had no acknowledged giver. None of the people said it was from them. It was a gift left unattached to anyone. It was a mystery. The turquoise was exactly like the one I found as a young child and became my prized possession. I gave it to the mystery warrior that saved my life and shared with me much wisdom."

"You are her Namesake; her name was a name not known to our ancestors an unknown name. I gave it to you . . . Mona."

Mona, took the necklace and but it around her neck once more. She solemnly swore: "It is my honor and pleasure to do as you have asked, it will be passed down through my children until our memories are just mist and the stone is the only solid connection to the past."

Seventy-five thousand years later, Captain Mona Ann Lisa Commander of the Mother Ship Dragonfly sat in her wardroom with two prized new crew members. She had just shown them still images of the exchange between Eva and her daughter Mona. All three had tears in their eyes.

The good Captain said: "The stone is the one Eva gave me before I left Earth. The difference now is it contains a quantum communications node. As long as the stone is with your bloodline, we will know their location and can monitor if necessary. As we do further research into human history, we may find it necessary to reengage. I am honored to be part of this remarkable lineage."

Love Defeats Death

Short Story 10
By George and Linda B

Eva and her daughter Mona must separate again due to the extreme weather changes making the area dryer and subject to continual wildfires. Eva and Toby decide to return to the Boneyard while Mona decided to stay in place.

Eva is distracted and deep in thought. She decided to divide the Boneyard Nation once again into two separate and independent groups. Again, this is for survival. Her memory goes back to her first decision that meant the loss of her parents when she was just a teenager and first appointed clan leader.

At least the last time she split the Nation and forced them away from the Boneyard hunting grounds, she was able to reunite after 20 cycles apart. In doing so over the last five years she saw her grandchildren grow into young adults.

In these few years Eva and her daughter worked hand and hand to keep as many alive as possible in the miserable heat, drought, wildfires and attack from marauding human and animal predators. She thanked the creator for finding her daughter after more than nineteen years apart. After five cycles together Eva was almost completely gray. Toby, her husband and second in command, was not the unshakable warrior he once was. Mona, Eva's daughter was still in her prime, but she had lost much in the last few years of strife and hardships. Her husband Flint, the Mammoth Clan leader, had been killed two cycles back. His Clan was now almost extinct because the massive herds of mammoths could not find pasture or enough water to sustain them against the relentless attack from human and megafauna predation. There numbers dwindled until only dead carcasses remained.

The last meeting between Eva, Toby and Mona resulted in decisions made from desperation and urgency. The two divisions of the Boneyard Nation were only a shadow of their peak numbers. The Elk Clan numbered only 200 and the Bison Clan maybe 250 in total. The last terror birds had died two cycles ago from disease and poor diet. The Clan leaders had lost almost everything except their children and their duties and responsibilities.

Unknown to Eva and Mona a very important meeting was being held thousands of years and millions of miles away. Captain Mona Ann Lisa and her science officers were in deep discussions. Two others were in attendance. These two were lower ranking members of the crew of the Dragonfly but had a deep and abiding stake in the outcome of the enclave. Rain Cloud and Sunrise listened intently and prayed the meeting would result in decisive action being taken. Moonbeam and Levie were arguing in favor of intervention. Mona on the other hand was reluctant but was strongly influenced by her brilliant sisters.

Mona had previously acted decisively twice before and doing so possibly risked all their futures if something had gotten screwed up. The fact they were having this discussion was proof their previous actions were successful.

The ancient surveillance drones were nearing their service life but were still functioning and were targeting the tiny turquoise stone worn by Mona, which was given to her by Eva, her mother. Originally, the stone was given to Captain Mona Ann Lisa by Eva when Eva was just a little girl. Captain Lisa anonymously returned the stone to Eva as a birthing gift to Eva when she was pregnant with Mona. Captain Lisa had the stone implanted with a tiny transmitter that emitted a constant tracking signal.

Two weeks had passed since the mother and daughter tribal leaders had made their fateful decision. The Clans split. After much grief, weeping and hugs the two meager human bans parted, suspecting they would never see each other again. This was both prophetic and tragically correct. Eva with Toby now walked away from their son, daughter, and grandchildren. This was inevitable, Mona could not morally or ethically as Clan Leader leave her people and go with her parents. Everyone knew they were all living on borrowed time. By dividing they were possibly only buying a few weeks of survival, but this was the only rational decision under the miserable circumstances.

Thousands of years later, the most powerful woman in two Galaxies has a strong seizure, within which she visualized a tragic end to her beloved Eva and Toby. Could she accept this emotional catastrophe or should she or could she change the inevitable? From the surveillance drones and mitochondrial DNA historical mutation analysis she knew Mona's Clan survived and later became a powerful and successful people group whose genetic progeny survive until Captain Mona's era and beyond. No such evidence exists for Eva and her half of the Boneyard Nation. They simply cease to exist, a dead end. And if her vision was correct, a very tragic end.

Captain Lisa was very disturbed and wanted to act; however, she had interfered twice already and as they say the third time is the charm. Could she really take such a risk; pushing not only her luck but risk the fate of the entire human race in the balance.

As the science enforcement authority on time travel and management, Mona could not break the rules she enforced. Whatever she did had to be completely above board and precise in execution. If she broke the rules, she could not face the blowback to her technical leadership, moral authority, and integrity. Never-the-less, she was now convinced she must do something. So, Captain Lisa called her sisters Moonbeam and Levie, the best scientists in the known universe, to devise a plan of action.

The sisters recounted the rules. One can only use physical time travel once to the same 4D coordinates (3D coordinates in space plus exact time). If one goes physically to a time and location one may only stay a few minutes and return, if they do not return quickly, they must remain where inserted for several days or more. Returning before a significant time delay results in a decompression like syndrome that is usually unavoidably fatal to the traveler. However, there is a technology perfected by the sisters referred to as the Shadowland Journey. This process allows a person to send their consciousness to a past or future time and location. They can observe but not interact physically with the physical environment. There are no observational limitations to this technology except; there are an infinite number of times and locations one could observe. To find the exact point in time and location turns out to be extremely difficult. The target is there but no one has adequate information to find the exact grain of sand in the desert.

To limit the search, the sisters have the information from the surveillance drones targeting Eva's daughter's gemstone. They knew Eva parted from Mona on a date in late spring. We also know her half of the Boneyard Nation went west, toward what is now known by our generation as Yellowstone National Park. The Sisters suspect Eva and Toby are leading their Clan toward the Boneyard hunting grounds. Noting they are on foot, pulling sleds and drags. They are without beasts of burden and are very weak and without supplies. They must hunt and scavenge as they travel. The Sisters fear they might not reach their goal and even if they did, the resources within the hunting grounds might be meager or nonexistent.

What happened to Earth? It is a complex solar system consisting of not one star, the sun, but three. One is a brown and one is a blue dwarf star. They pass near the sun in an elliptical orbit every so many thousands of years. When they do the amount of tectonic disturbance of earth varies dramatically from very mild to catastrophic. Even mild disturbance can lead to local environmental disruption that can cause extinctions of surface flora and fauna. This last pass caused the super volcano under Yellowstone (the Boneyard) to erupt significantly enough to disrupt the entire ecosystem of North America.

Toby's mind is cloudy, it is hard to maintain focus. Eva is now riding on his back. Her deformed foot is causing her much distress. His exhaustion is very high in his weakened state. His mind wanders to the first time he saw Eva. He was her prisoner, tied to a tree with two of his companions. She looked directly into his eyes and instead of hate directed toward an enemy he saw wisdom and kindness. She was a beautiful and diminutive female with a distinctive limp. In his young life he had never been this close to a woman. He had been taken from his mother soon after he had been weaned and trained to be a warrior without the right to think for himself or freedom except to kill as he chose anyone or anything the Strong man designated as an enemy of the Fanatics. He took orders and knew the only way to find a life mate was to rise in the command structure of the Strong Man's lieutenants. Only one in fifty warriors reached this level.

When Eva freed him, he chose to stay with her people instead of returning to the cruelty of the Fanatics. He helped her drive the Strong Man from the Boneyard hunting grounds and finally became her highest-ranking warrior. The day he asked for her hand in marriage was the scariest and most joyful day of his life. Now he had to acknowledge all previous challenges, other humans or animal predators could not defeat them, but mother nature had signed their death warrants. He was not a defeatist but a realist. He saw no way out of their present dilemma. No game, no plant food sources, little or no water. Nature had turned against them all. He would fight to the end, but the end was so near he could taste it. They were now ten days journey since they left their daughter's settlement. Their daughter's people were no better than their Clan but were not exerting the effort to travel.

He collapsed dislodging Eva from his back. They fell and neither moved for hours. To his amazement no other clansmen were to be seen. In his stupor and desire to continue he must have left the others behind. He now had no energy to search for them. He sat half conscious and then slipped into oblivion. With Eva by his side, they were probably taking their last breaths.

Captain Mona Ann Lisa left the Time Management Council with approval for insertion of one individual to a narrowly defined time window to Mother Earth. The 4D coordinates allowed were based on the last known recording where Eva and Toby separated from Mona's camp. Captain Lisa would go alone. She had permission to have the observation drones locate on her and no longer target Mona's transmitter. She had a ten-day window to observe and take corrective action if possible. She was authorized to rescue only two persons. These individuals must not, at the time of rescue, be able to survive themselves and not be capable of assisting any other person to survive. Otherwise, their removal could result in changing history and thus sending a transformational ripple throughout eternity.

Captain Lisa was both excited and apprehensive. Could they locate Eva and Toby, and could they time the rescue such that all the Time Management Rules would be followed precisely? They had only one chance to succeed. Once attempted they could never return to these 4D coordinates again.

Moonbeam and Levie along with Rain Cloud and Sunrise met with Captain Lisa for hours planning an intricate mission. Rain Cloud and Sunrise were antiquity experts, in fact they were past members of the Boneyard Clan and Eva's parents.

The Sisters suggest several Shadowland missions before they even consider scheduling Captain Lisa's physical insertion into the timeline. So, Mona with Eva's parents went to the quiet lab to prepare for the first mission. They went to the same room and laid down in the reclining chairs. The Sisters put the earphones on all three and began the countdown. Within thirty seconds all three were unconscious.

As each awakened Mona spoke to them telepathically. Telling them to lock hands and glide with her to the 4D coordinates that were chosen for them by the Sisters.

They crossed space and time like it was not there and found themselves above Mona's encampment. It was early morning, and they could tell already that the heat was intense. Eva and Toby were saying their final farewells to Mona and her Children. Eva's son stayed with his sister; he too hugged and kissed his parents, goodbye.

Captain Lisa and Eva's parents were very moved by the events they were witnessing. They knew better than anyone Eva and Toby would never see their children and grandchildren again. Eva and Toby went to the front of their Clan and led them out of the camp towards the west and toward the Boneyard hunting grounds. Within an hour as the dust dissipated the Clans forever lost contact.

The first day of travel was the most productive. They covered at least fifteen miles. Each succeeding day they covered less and less territory. By the eighth day, most clansmen had already fallen behind and were incapable of going further. Mona and her shadowland companions watch in horror as the sick, weak, and starving people died by the dozens. They could not go back, more and more collapsing with each step. Toby and Eva could do nothing but lead forward. Eva probably would have died as well if it were not for Toby carrying her on his back.

On the ninth day Toby was the only person still moving. He did not look back and he did not stop, until he too collapsed. At that moment Captain Lisa left Eva's parents observing in Shadowland and awoke herself in the quiet lab. She jumped from the reclining chair and rushed to the time insertion module. She stripped off her clothes and ordered the module set to the 4D coordinates she had just left in Shadowland. This was for all the marbles. She had to land near her rescue subjects. She then had to cover both with her body and activate the retrieval protocol. This had to be done in less than three minutes or she had to remain on planet earth for several more days to prevent a fatal case of time reversal decompression.

Mona had done this exact thing once before when she rescued Rain Cloud and Sunrise. However, when she prevented Eva's assassination Captain Lisa remained on Planet for several months.

This time things went wrong. Toby aroused and became delirious, he saw Mona as an attacker. Though weak and disoriented he was a formidable opponent.

Captain Lisa had no time to explain or argue with Toby. She picked up a rock and attempted to clobber him. She was amazed by his speed and agility. He blocked her attack and kicked her legs from under her. Mona fell and struck her head momentarily stunning her. Wow! What a mess, she was running out of time. Did she avoid Toby completely and dive for Eva, removing her from certain death and leaving Toby to die alone? Or did she just commit to stay for several days. Naked and without weapons could she survive and care for her two charges until she could get them all off the Earth. She was sick at her stomach, she always allowed for every contingency. Not this time, how stupid could she have been?

Before she could blink her eyes one of the small surveillance drones swooped down and smashed into Toby's head. Toby fell immediately, totally unconscious. Mona still wobbling went to Eva and drug her next to Toby's prostrate carcass. She fell across both of them and initiated the retrieval process. Next thing she remembered she was waking up in her medical facility with a thermal blanket covering her naked body. What a headache! She tried to sit up but fell back down. A medical attendant immediately applied a sedative and Mona crashed again.

When Captain Lisa finally came around Moonbeam and Levie were standing over her with big smiles. In unison they both said, "Welcome back to the living."

Mona tried to smile but it hurt. So, she mumbled: "Who crashed the drone into Toby?"

Moonbeam very reluctantly raised her hand. Mona responded, "Good aim and good situational awareness. Thanks!" Levie protested, "It was my idea!"

Mona mumbled, "Well, thanks to both of you."

The two Sisters lifted Mona off the gurney and escorted her to her wardroom. When in private, she asked for all the details she missed while unconscious. The girls kept interrupting each other repeatedly talking over the other one. What Mona got was a frenetic tail which included the following. Toby will need reconstructive surgery on his face. Eva will be in a medically induced coma along with Toby for at least two weeks. They were outfitting one of the biospheres to resemble the Terror Bird Breeding Basin of the Boneyard. They thought it was best not to introduce them to Eva's parents until significant acclimation to their new world was accomplished.

Four weeks later, Captain Lisa went to the biosphere occupied by her rescued couple. Eva was removing bandages from Toby's head and face. They were sitting near a campfire in front of a crude shelter made from wood, tree branches, leaves, and moss. Mona neared the couple and calmly spoke in their language. "May I approach your camp and talk?"

Startled Eva turned, looked at Mona and with a puzzled look said: "Yes, but do I know you? And where are we? I thought we had died!"

Mona collected herself and made short statements of fact. "Yes, you know me. I visited you when you were but a child. You are far from dead, and you are many, many, cycles, and miles from where you were just three weeks ago. You are now above the sky you looked up into and are beyond the stars you use to see at night."

Eva asked, "How did we get here?"

Mona responded, "That is a confusing story. and it would not make much sense to you now; however, we will tell you when you can comprehend its complexity. Until then we are going to assign two people to answer your questions and help you adjust here."

Mona then signaled for Rain Cloud and Sunrise to approach. Eva's and Toby's hair had already returned to the color of their youth. Though they were unaware it had happened. Toby's eyes had been covered with bandages and Eva had no mirror to see her youthful appearance. Eva felt much better but had not put anything into perspective yet. As her parents approached, they too were youthful and healthy. She did not recognize them, but did think they could have been from her Clan.

Her father spoke first, "Welcome to your new home and people. We are here to teach you many new things and stand by you, and we hope to become your new family."

Eva thought, *she had just left her children, grandchildren and lost her people. How could she just start again with strangers and people who were not her family. How could this man be so presumptuous?* Mona sensing the pain in Eva's eyes stepped in between the two.

Mona knew Eva was close to disassembling and was stressed beyond measure. The Captain simply pointed something out obviously unacknowledged. Mona pointed to Eva's leg and foot and asked if she knew it was no longer deformed? Eva's mouth dropped open and looked down to see she no longer had a clubbed foot. How could she have missed such a thing? Stunned, dumbstruck and speechless, her eyes teared up. She turned to Toby and burrowed her face into his broad chest. She cried uncontrollably for minutes. All her pent-up emotions held in for months and maybe years were unleashed. Mona motioned Eva's parents to follow her away from the couple. They would return after this emotional storm was spent.

Mona understood Eva. This woman was so strong and remarkable, she had no equal. Things need to go slow, there was no rush. Time was not an issue. If it took years to acclimate Eva, she was more than worth the effort.

Mona ordered the pair to be left alone until Toby or Eva asked for someone to interact with them.

Several weeks later Captain Lisa was summoned by her honored guests to the biosphere. Mona was both elated and apprehensive. She desperately wanted to have a significant relationship with these remarkable ancestors. How they had survived impossible odds, carving out the moral and ethical foundations of a culture that still existed in Mona's time. The Code of Conduct which has been ratified by trillions of sentient beings across thousands of galaxies can be traced through the remnant of the human species back to Eva and Toby. Their ethical treatment of humans and animals alike passed forward generation after generation has reaped untold benefits for thousands and thousands of years.

Eva welcomed Mona into their camp. Unlike before (when she wore primitive clothes matching her guests) Mona wore her work uniform. This was a one-piece gray body suit not unlike a wet suit used in scuba diving. Her rank and ship insignia were displayed on her shoulders and on the front of her suit. This was a first time reveal to her guests. To her surprise the couple did not react negatively.

Eva motioned for Mona to sit with them near the fire. There were furs scattered on the ground for their comfort. Eva started the conversation. "I know you, you are Mona, whose name I gave my daughter. You were with me for some time when I was very young." Mona nodded yes. "You came in my dreams later and gave me ideas and encouraged me to experiment with healing and weapons, and tactics. Are Toby and I alive? Are we prisoners? Why are we here?"

Mona replied: "You are very alive; you are not prisoners but under our care at this time. The two of you are my family. However, we are separated by at least 2,000 generations. I am basically your daughter. Within my genetic code is the memory of your life and all those that lived between you and me. I have Toby's memories as well encoded within my body's DNA. We call it genetic memory. With our technology we can unravel this record. Your memories are the first found, there are no others before yours. For some reason we cannot decipher why this is true. We find no memory code before you and Toby. For example, we have no encoded memory from your parents. There must be an explanation. We think this has to do with the catastrophic cycle and cosmic energy surges that the Earth experienced soon after your birth. This destructive cycle finally culminated in your Clan's horrible fate. Like you, I inherited some paranormal abilities. I have premonitions and visions. I feel the Creator gave us these abilities to accomplish things others are unable to do."

Eva asked, "What will become of us?"

"That is up to you. You are free to do as you wish. Just know we are here to help you discover a new existence. In fact, we have done this before with people from your era in human history. I would like to introduce them to you now if you would like."

Toby spoke for the first time with a big smile, "I would like that very much!"

"We tried to do this earlier, but you were simply not ready. I would like to introduce two distinguished members of our crew." Two young looking but mature people walked out of the shadows toward the campfire. "Eva, this is Rain Cloud and Sunrise, your parents. They will be helping the two of you start your new life."

Eva collapsed, fainting for the first time in her life.

Sue Meets ManKiller

Short Story 11
Taken from: Volume 1, Mona Lisa on the Moon,
Thirty-Two Thousand Years in the Making
By George B

D r. Sue Grammar, professor of antiquities and World Alliance War Planning Committee member, was balled up in a tight fetal position in the shower stall of her private apartment, considering thoughts of suicide.

Sue screamed to herself, "What the heck did I do? Sure, be a patriot! Step up and be the mother of a new civilization. Save humankind from extinction. I believed my own trite propaganda. I volunteered for this—first in line to be permanently modified, this sucks!"

Note: Sue was having menstrual cramps. Cramps are the scourge of woman every month and have been since the great global war some thirty-two thousand years ago. Before the genetically engineered change, women had one ovulation per year; now, of course, in the twenty-first century, women ovulate once a month. Sue had been in an underground shelter for five months. This shelter was designed for the leaders of the World Alliance to maintain communication with the assumed surviving assets of the dwindling fighters. It was coincidence she was there at all. Sue was simply on a tour with other War Planning Committee members when the first Atlantis Alliance strike literally obliterated SpaceJump City. Over three million people died on the surface in a matter of seconds. She knew she was a lucky woman, though in much mental and internal agony. She had volunteered to be the first female genetically modified to ovulate each month a painful personal price paid to increase the birth rate. It could be said Sue was having second thoughts about her decision.

Jim Jimmerson from the Space Legal Counsel's Office knocked on Dr. Grammar's door.

Jim asked, "Sue, are you available for a meeting with the War Planning Committee? We are updating all the status reports."

"Yeah, sure, give me a minute," Sue replied. She thought to herself, *Wow! my abdominal cavity feels like ... like ... No words can explain ... Jeez!*

She then said, "Jim, I'll meet you there in five minutes."

"Okay, Sue. They are anxious to talk about phase three of the war plan." Sue collected herself, put on the shelter-designated jumpsuit, and proceeded to the conference facility.

When Sue walked in, everyone was seated in two rows facing a wall-sized image screen. Sue found a seat in the back row as the meeting began. Jim Jimmerson was standing to one side of the screen and began speaking. "Members of the War Planning Committee, it appears 99 percent of the hostilities have ended. The toll to our alliance and to the Atlantis Alliance is staggering. Of the estimated human Earth population of some five hundred million, our projections indicate an 80 percent death rate, with 50 percent more of the survivors expected to perish in the next six weeks, meaning that only fifty million people are projected to be alive at that time. Are there any questions so far?" Jim continued. "Ecological destruction is almost as staggering. It is estimated there has been a 70 percent loss of life-sustaining ecosystems on the land surfaces and a 40 percent loss in a composite of all aquatic environments. In most areas of the globe, the climate will change from the previous norms into a nuclear winter phase that will move the ice sheets to extremes never before seen on Earth's surface. Unless we shelter and protect selected groups of survivors, humans will become almost extinct on the surface. These conditions could last from one hundred to one thousand years, depending on location, and in some cases it could last forever. On the positive side, we have learned the following: Many of the apex predators that prey on humans have also died. The Atlantis Alliance is no longer a threat to humanity, and the Black Magicians have all been eliminated, primarily because of their own arrogance. Our underground and underwater shelters are operational and functioning."

Sue was shocked at the status of the world she had known and loved. She might never again see or hear from her dear friend Mona, Mona's parents, or, of course, her boyfriend from the AA. All she knew was that she still had duties to perform and now children to make and raise to preserve the species. At least the sick leadership of the Atlantis Alliance had been eliminated—but at such a dear, dear cost to all of humanity. When the meeting was ending, she was recognized as the single person most responsible for the demise of the Black Magicians and their Aryan super-race agenda. Her fact-gathering, land survey research, and ancient language skills had given the World Alliance the critical pieces of the puzzle that gave them the edge needed to defeat the AA. With one hand, she had helped to destroy; and now with the other hand, she would have to build a new future for the human race. But right now, all she could feel was the cramps in her abdomen. "When the heck are these going to stop?" she said to herself.

Later, Dr. Sue Grammar was sitting at her desk in the underground shelter near what used to be the wilderness surrounding SpaceJump City. She could not even imagine the horrors that were being played out on the surface of Earth on every continent. Humans, animals, and plant life were being tested to their limits. At some point, the war council was going to send recon teams to look for survivors once the firestorms had sufficiently subsided. Survivors would either be assisted in place or moved to shelters with any capacity. Sue resolved she would volunteer for the first team whenever it went out.

When Sue found out the war council was about to send out its first teams to the surface, she rushed to the transportation bay, where the personnel were assembling for departure. As she arrived, she was met by her friend Jim of the Space Legal Counsel's Office. Jim asked, "Where do you think you're going?"

"To the surface with the recon team, of course," said Sue.

"I don't think so."

Sue turned her back and proceeded toward the craft yelling back. "Why not?"

"Well, I can think of several logical reasons, but the best one is that you are too valuable to the war planning council to risk death or injury up there."

Sue was adamant. "I am no better than anyone else; I need to go, Jim."

"Well, if you won't listen to reason, there is the legal contract you signed, which prohibits any activities that could reasonably result in death or injury."

With a confused stare Sue said, "What in the devil are you talking about? I was never restricted before … heck, I was one of the first people on the ground at Mount Olympus."

"When you volunteered for the permanent ovulation frequency modification, it was in the fine print."

"Good Grief! When you need a lawyer, you can't find one, and when you don't want one, one is in your face," Sue said with keen frustration.

Sue Grammar was furious about being denied the chance to go with the recon team to the surface. She said to herself, "Do you for one minute think some contract small print will keep me from doing what I know I need to do?" She had heard the recon team had to stand down because of some maintenance issue with the vertical-takeoff-and-landing rescue craft. So, when the team left for some coffee, she crawled aboard and hid in the rescue gear below deck. The vehicle launched about two hours later, and Sue was getting cramped and beaten up by the gear, which was not tied down well. The ride was very violent, with frequent sharp banks and turns. She could smell terrible odors, and the heat was extremely uncomfortable. What made it worse was the fact she could see nothing from her hiding place below deck. About an hour into the mission, the craft began a steep descent and then pulled up violently. That was the last thing she remembered.

When Sue woke up, she was in pain. She could see through the cracks in the craft's frame; she could see a red glow in the distance but no sounds. The air was very hard to breathe, and the temperature was high. She had no idea how long she had been there, what time of day it was, or where she was. She thought she might have bitten the big one this time. Throughout her life, she had always done risky things and lived to tell the story. She felt her luck might have run out this time. She tried to move, but the pain prevented much more than a small readjustment of her arms. She was trapped in the crumpled cargo hold of a crashed rescue craft. She thought to herself, *So, who rescues the crew of a rescue craft that is trying to rescue the survivors of the war to end all wars?* It didn't look good, even to a wisecracking eternal optimist.

Mankiller, the alpha male of a wolf pack roaming the wilderness in the Late Pleistocene, had a mission. His world had been turned upside down by the war between two packs of humans. Mankiller was ancient; he remembered when men first encroached into his hunting grounds. They brought in technology, making his coordinated attacks ineffective; he had to retreat farther and farther into the depths of the wilderness to protect his progeny. Gone now were the automated sensors and traps that kept them far from humans. His pack could have easily hunted the remaining Pleistocene megafauna after the war because many were crippled and vulnerable. This was not Mankiller's desire; he wanted human prey. They had already found some human survivors and dispatched them quickly, not even stopping to feed. They were obsessed with the blood sport, acting more human than animal now.

Sue, more desperate than ever, had begun to yell for help and struggle to free herself from the material pinning her down. Mankiller instinctively became alerted on hearing Sue's crying. The pack topped the hill and saw the wreckage below. The craft was ruptured and badly damaged in the front. On quick inspection from a distance, Mankiller saw no movement in or around the craft. Apparently, the surviving crew had either been picked up by a rescue craft themselves or had left on foot. The only clue that life was present was Sue's yelling for help.

Sue heard something coming from outside, but there were no voices … she immediately sensed danger and stopped crying and struggling. Holding her breath, she looked around in the dim light for anything that looked like a weapon. She saw just out of her reach a flare gun in a holster and the explosive flare canisters attached to the web belt on the holster's sides. She had to reach it.

Mankiller set his pack to digging around the base of the craft, where he could see a rupture. He could smell the fear being generated inside and started to howl. The bloodlust was driving him now more than ever.

Back at the alliance underground shelter, Jim was reviewing the after-action recon report, which detailed how the first craft had to make an emergency crash landing. All crew members were later picked up with only minor injuries. He was so happy he had prevented Sue Grammar from going on the mission. He couldn't wait to tell Sue "I told you so!" at the next planning meeting.

Sue began feeling with her free hands for something to reach the webbed belt. With each movement, a pain exploded in her left side. She bit her lips to remain as quiet as possible. Through a wide crack in the bulkhead, she saw for the first time the eyes of the apex predator. She knew immediately that being quiet was no longer necessary. Sue yelled and tried with all her strength to lunge for the flare gun. Her adrenaline now surged, and her pain was drowned by her desperation. To her surprise, her hands reached the belt and she pulled herself out of the material pinning her down. Sue pulled the gun out of the holster, opened it by breaking it into the familiar L shape she recalled from her survival training, and put a flare canister in the breech. *Now what? Good Grief! This canister is designed to fly fifteen hundred feet into the air and ignite while floating slowly down, attached to a small parachute. If I shoot it in this enclosed space, I might be the only casualty!*

Mankiller could see the human female caged in the wreck. He could feel her fear but sensed her resolve and intelligence. He realized this might not be the routine kill he and his pack of predators had recently become accustomed to.

The floor in the front portion of the storage hold had peeled back on itself like the sole of an old shoe ripped from its threads and creased, the front half lying under the back half. Sue, seeing Mankiller's eyes through a wide crack, could hear the pack digging in the hard earth to get under the metal bulkhead in the front of the compartment. The only thing between them and Sue was a few feet of earth and about twenty feet of cluttered space between the front of the hold and where Sue was barricaded up against the wall in the back. Sue's mind was racing. The door behind her had been jammed shut in the crash, and there was no way out. She would eventually have to use the flare gun or allow the wolves a free meal.

A flash came to Sue's demented mind: ***Professor of Antiquities Found Half-Baked in Makeshift Dutch Oven; Was Delightful Meal for Passing Pack of Hungry Wolves.*** *Wow! Where do I get these ideas!*

Sue watched in horror as several paws became visible, digging frantically under the metal bulkhead in the front of the hold. Sue had to react quickly. "Well, guess I need to time this perfectly."

Once the canister is fired, there is a pause between the launch and the ignition of the flare. I can either try to target one animal with the canister or just fire before the group gets in and hope the heat from the flare will discourage them. *Maybe, just maybe, I can reload and get another round off.* Sue could see Mankiller getting closer to the craft, his eyes staring into hers, looking through the wide breach. He was enjoying the thought of ripping this human female apart while she was still alive and screaming. Sue picked up the flare gun with both hands and aimed at the area where the paws were digging. She thought, *At least I don't have to experience any more of those infernal cramps every month!*

She then suddenly turned and fired through the large fissure in the bulkhead, hitting Mankiller square in the chest. He fell back as the canister's propellant drove the flare casing deep into his body. Sue immediately reloaded and fired toward the paws under the front bulkhead. The last thing she experienced was the flash of the flare and the intense heat from the phosphorus.

Sue was smiling to herself, thinking she had gotten the last laugh on the ancient Mankiller. Was she dead? Where was the tunnel of light? She had a list of things to do when she died; one was to look up her old boyfriend from the Atlantis Alliance. She had been told when she was young that one got a perfect body after one died. She couldn't wait to see if her tattoo was missing.

Silver returned to the laboratory to look in on Sue Grammar. Silver was wearing her ancient garb with a bow over her shoulder and a quiver of arrows. She had earlier brought Sue to the lab, unconscious but very alive, and briefed the Doctors Ben and Peggy Lisa on what had happened. Peggy could never figure out why a woman named Silver had such red hair. Silver's companion, an elvish blond young man, was by her side. Sue looked up at Silver and asked if there was a costume party going on. Silver laughed, and the man just turned and left.

Peggy then asked, "Silver, how did you find Sue and know where to look?"

Silver responded, "Our prophets foretold of Sue's coming ordeal with Mankiller and the Guardianship's need for her knowledge. The quantum sight led us to the downed rescue craft. Sue is an exceptionally strong person; few others would have survived until we got there. She will make an excellent addition to the Prometheus Council."

"Ouch! That freaking hurt!" She said to herself. Someone was sticking an IV needle in her left arm and shining a bright light in her left eye. This was not a good sign. She was liking the idea of being dead.

"Wake up, Sue. Wake up. You, okay?" It was a voice from the past.

"Heck no! Leave me be!" Sue yelled, still in shock. When Sue was able to focus her vision, she saw a man and woman that looked like Mona's parents. Now I know I'm dead. Ben and Peggy Lisa went missing from the Moon Research Center along with Moonbeam before SpaceJump City went up in smoke.

"Sue, drink some water; it will help you come around," said Peggy. Sue was still semiconscious.

"I don't want to come around; are you some kind of sadist?" Sue then realized that Ben and Peggy were there to welcome her to heaven. That must be it! "Ben, Peggy, it is so sweet for the two of you to welcome me. Is Mona here too … is she?" Sue smiled.

Peggy quickly responded, "No dear."

Sue, ever jovial, said, "So this is the holding area for heaven? When do you take me for a quick tour?"

Ben chimed in. "You are under the ocean, not heaven."

"Okay, you are kidding, aren't you? I'm dead, and so are both of you, right? There is no way I could have escaped that pack of wolves." Sue was starting to come around fully.

Back at the alliance shelter, Jim finally figured out Sue was missing. It became immediately apparent she was a stowaway on the first rescue mission. The alliance immediately launched a mission to locate Sue. They found the downed craft surrounded by ten dead wolves, seven of which had arrows in their bodies. One, the largest, was nearest to a large hole cut into the side of the storage hold from the outside in. The large wolf had been burned to ashes from his chest forward. There was no Sue. A search was made for several miles in a grid surrounding the ruined craft. The search was then called off. Someone they didn't know had most likely taken Sue.

Dr. Sue Grammar, professor of antiquities and member of the World Alliance War-Planning Council, dispatcher of Mankiller, and future initiate of the Prometheus Council, was beginning to get her sea legs back under her. Ever ready to make a wisecrack, she began to inquire seriously about her surroundings. "Since I am not dead, why in the world am I here?"

Ben spoke first, stating, "Well, you see Sue, we have this puzzle given to us from the first human concubine of Prometheus, and you might be the key to solving the darn thing. Did I mention that if we don't, the world could end?"

Sue, ever the scientist and comic, stated, "Let me see … concubine, Prometheus, puzzle, me—the world could end. Is that about, right? Excuse me, but methinks the world has come to an end. So, what is there left to save? Well, Ben, I just spent the afternoon with a canine with one bad attitude, not to mention a few of his buddies. So, you might want to go a bit slower so my brain can catch up."

Peggy understood and said, "Oh, let me do it, Ben." She took over. "What do you know of the Voynich manuscript? Could it have an encrypted coded message within its contents?" Sue knew Peggy was serious.

"It could." Peggy responded.

"How do we find out? We have less than two years to figure this thing out."

"Okay, I'm willing to help! But can I eat first? Please!" Sue seemed to be hungrier than concerned about the fate of the world. After Sue ate about a pound of boiled shrimp, a three-pound steamed lobster, and three cups of kelp and sea urchin soup, she was ready to listen and talk. "I once did some deep looking into this ancient manuscript," Sue said. "There was always significant debate over its age and contents. It appears to be a catalog of plants that don't exist, in exquisite detail, and other nonsensical stuff. Point being, we were looking into the possibility it was a code book of sorts. At the time, we didn't have a tool like Moonbeam to help us parse it out. Since Moonbeam is part of our investigation team, I am confident we can break into its secrets—especially since we know for a fact of its specific age and origin. Yes, these were confirmed by Prometheus's significant other. Take it from me; it gets no more confirmed than that!"

Jim was devastated. The alliance had just lost their most capable scientist and leader, not to mention their best comedian. The evidence left at the crash scene suggested several things. Sue had been trapped in the lower cargo hold of the rescue craft. That was where she hid to avoid being prevented from going on the first rescue mission from the secure underground facilities of the alliance. Analysis of the evidence at the crash scene was strange, to say the least. A forensic analysis of the dead wolf pack revealed some obvious specifics. The animal nearest to the hole cut into the exterior of the craft had most likely been killed by being struck by a flare gun canister. Based on his size and assumed age, he was thought to be the alpha male and, of course, pack leader. The canister was fired from within the hold, most assuredly by Sue. The two wolves in front of the hold just outside the interior of the craft were burned beyond analysis. The remaining seven had been killed by arrows, which remained in their bodies. Whoever did this must have been expert archers and marksmen because only two different footprints were found. The arrows were of superior grade and construction, but ancient in design. Jim swore he would find Sue if it was humanly possible.

Captain Lisa versus Gilda the Evil Cloud Queen

Short Story 12
An Excerpt from "Volume 1, Mona Lisa on the Moon,
Thirty-Two Thousand Years in the Making"

Gilda the Cloud Queen of the Swarm was the Uncontested Leader of Thirty Billion Scavengers. In contrast to Mona's preparation, Gilda's consisted of eating fewer desserts. She was so confident of her victory that she didn't even consider a strategy in the unlikely chance she lost. Without question, her arrogance was one of her best qualities. Without such extreme hubris, she would have been just one of the dull queens in the Swarm's history. Gilda craved adulation, fame, and eternal renown. She fantasized this competition being immortalized as an epic battle between the greatest queen ever and the upstart alien aided by the treasonous shock troop commander. To guarantee her place as a living legend, not only did Gilda need to crush CapHead and Mona, but she had to make sure they were considered formidable threats. The queen was feeling rather good presently in the months since the Succession Challenge made by CapHead the Supreme Commander of Tribe II and the human upstart Captain Mona Ann Lisa. They had sustained no more mysterious attacks in months, and since she had sent the amphibians away from the swarm, she had been in total control except for Mona's insolence and the traitorous CapHead's act on the cloud wide communication link eight months ago. The queen was now four hundred years old and had reigned for at least one hundred years. She was young because cloud queens historically didn't get the chance to rule this soon, owing to the long lifespans of the queens-in-waiting in line ahead of them. This was not a problem for Gilda; she took things into her own hands and assisted Mother Nature a tad. No one really connected the dots, but four of the more senior candidates died way too young. Gilda just smiled and mourned the untimely death of her noble competition. Fair play was never in Gilda's play-book. The queen knew they were within days of dumping the amphibians and hoped it would be timed perfectly so the creature Mona and her King Hopeful CapHead would see the act personally. This Queen had no need of a king and never would have appointed one, but she had a short list just in case. She grudgingly had to admit that CapHead was at the top of the list. This made Mona's challenge even more delicious; Gilda was going to get revenge times two. To CapHead the diminutive human female Captain Mona Ann Lisa was as formidable an adversary as he had ever encountered. He was not only beginning to respect Mona but was enjoying her as well. He had always despised the present cloud queen, as most of the other supreme tribal leaders did. The queen was unreasonably brutal even among the most ruthless culture in the galaxy. If things had to change, CapHead could see no other way for it to happen. This was going to be an exciting and bumpy ride into the unknown. His fighting nature was engaged, and he was anxious for the next phase to begin. Bring it on!

Mona still had a few months before the competition, and she was training hard under CapHead's supervision. CapHead told Mona the queen's name was Gilda and that this knowledge might be used against her at the right moment. The rules of the competition mandated that each contestant be wired with a voice connection that neither could turn off. He felt the queen would verbally harass Mona constantly, so he would train her to ignore it. He, however, suggested that Mona withhold her verbal counterattacks on Gilda for the right moment, when they could be decisive. The queen's uncontrollable temper was her most glaring weakness.

The competition would be held in the largest biosphere in the collective. The sphere was presently near the power sphere but would be moving to the outer strata of vessels to take advantage of more and more infrared radiation as they neared the central star of this solar system. The contained ecosystem was equivalent to about twenty square miles of continuous variable terrain. Her familiarity with it gave Gilda even more confidence of success. CapHead was familiar with the terrain in the biosphere, and with Moonbeam's and Levie's assistance, and with information extracted from Chaos's spying, they recreated much of it in 3-D imaging in the ore holds on Dragonfly. Mona was going to be much more familiar with the existing terrain and its flora and fauna than the cloud queen herself. CapHead especially worked with Mona on hiding places, where she could be much more effectively concealed than the much larger cloud queen. Each contestant had to submit schematics of the two weapons they were allowed to bring to the competition. If approved, these weapons could be fabricated and inspected the day of competition by their seconds. CapHead was Mona's designated second. All other weapons were supplied by the officials based on the specific characteristics of the five trials. Mona sent schematics of her bow and arrows. She also submitted schematics of a boomerang. The cloud queen sent schematics of a large dagger and an extra-large javelin. The boomerang appeared to be just an L-shaped cutting tool to CapHead, and he asked why she might want it. After Mona demonstrated its use, he smiled from ear to ear. Both teams approved the weapons. CapHead never said exactly why, but he stressed conditioning above all else to Mona. She was running around the ore holds for hours each day, climbing up and down walls and ladders, and swimming underwater for long distances. He had her conditioning at high simulated altitudes for long periods of time. If she asked why, he just said the swarm's advance scouts and shock troops were under his leadership for a reason.

Gilda thought she should do some weapons training since it was now less than thirty days to the competition. She had to pick a second but genuinely trusted no one. She was trying to think whose family she had in prison and could therefore trust would not fail her for fear of death or torture visited on their loved ones. *Oh yes!* she thought to herself, *Supreme Tribal Leader IX. I had his mother thrown in prison for telling that joke about me at that state banquet ten years ago. He should do very well.* She called her bodyguards and had them retrieve IX's mother from prison. Next, she summoned IX for an audience.

A three-hundred-page document had been received by Mona and CapHead three days ago detailing the rules and obligations of the succession competition. Jim had been going over it and was about to brief everyone on its provisions and responsibilities. Just by looking at Jim, one could see he had a headache. Sue asked, "What in this solar system are all the details about?" Silver just smiled, knowing that after 115,000 years, she was about to hear something new. Jim rubbed his head and read some provisions:

- Winner takes responsibility for the loser's families (no significant torture or imprisonments allowed.) Confiscation of all property is allowed, however, and removal of all property rights to the third generation is permissible.
- Winner must cremate or bury challenger and second's bodies or consume them at celebratory banquet.
- The loser's tribe will forfeit all seniority in succession for three hundred years or until two cloud queens have been replaced, whichever comes first.
- Losers' names will not be allowed to be spoken for two hundred years, and those with the same names will have them legally changed by the courts.
- For the games to begin, the mother and father of the competitors must be present at the start of competition (or their designated legally sufficient replacement) and held by the game officials so the winner may later have them placed in stocks and ridiculed during the celebratory banquet afterward.

C. E. interjected. "That last provision is a killer. We would never want Ben and Peggy there, even if they could get here in the time remaining. It is impossible."

Jim said, "The line '(or their designated legally sufficient replacement)' means that Mona can substitute a male and female whom the queen will accept as people she would like to belittle and ridicule upon Mona's death and dismemberment. Any volunteers?"

"Count me in," said C. E., Silver, and Sue, but Mona eliminated Silver because she would be second in command upon Mona's death.

Sue said, "I guess it is you and me, big guy. I always wanted to be a mom."

Mona asked, "Are you two sure about this?"

Sue declared, "Sure. I can't wait to see this biosphere thingy."

C. E. agreed that he would love to see it as well … up close and personal. Mona was getting really annoyed by this game she was training for. It was one thing for her and CapHead to risk everything, but the involvement of Sue and C. E. was a complication she had not bargained for. Defeating this cloud queen was going to get all her attention from this point on. She asked CapHead to double their training schedule until the event. C. E. and Sue had up to this time not really talked that much. Both respected each other's abilities, but they had not really had a personal conversation.

C. E. asked, "Sue, just how did you meet Mona anyway?"

Sue replied, "The meeting was simple; the relationship is more complicated, as it developed over the years. Mona was a student of mine. She was the youngest to be in my course on ancient antiquities ever. Really, she was a child prodigy. At first, I thought she was like other overly bright kids, but was I wrong. She never got lost, stayed focused on her studies, and had no problem seeing the big picture. Her intuition and personal skills were off the charts. When she went into space engineering years later, we bumped into each other and became friends. I met her parents before they shipped off to a long-term position at the Moon Research Center, and I guess I became her older sister and the extended earthbound family she never had. How very ironic it is that if it had not been for my relationship with Mona, I would not be here but would be dead and forgotten like most of the human species. So, no matter what happens, I am on Mona's team, come hell or high water."

C. E. interjected. "From what I have seen in the short time I have been privileged to be around her; I agree completely. My first encounter with Mona was in my position as senior crew chief on the Space Search and Rescue Team administration. As a pilot candidate, she was required to spend weeks flying missions with our teams in near-earth situations. I can tell you I saw none better. In fact, she was so good that when they launched the WAMS Dragonfly, I attended the launch ceremony. That was the first and only launch ceremony I ever attended in person. I just wanted to see that exceptional person take possession of that magnificent creation, the Dragonfly. How ironic that I am now presently on the Dragonfly. And I agree with you I am proud to serve with you as one of Mona's substitute parents. How about a drink to celebrate?"

CapHead agreed to increase the training pace but did not want to push Mona too far, as he knew he could destroy her frail human physiology. However, it seemed that no matter what he metered out, she exceeded his expectations. He was beginning to believe they might not become Gilda's midnight snack after all. Whatever happened, he was having a great time working with a being (other than a fellow scavenger) that he didn't despise. He really didn't understand why Mona had not only spared his life and given back his eyesight but was also trusting him with her very survival. The only thing he could say was that he wanted more than anything he had wanted in a very long time to see a non-scavenger defeat and destroy one of his own. Mona was in her training mode—the one she had fallen into before for the World Games not so many years prior. She had experienced this frequently when she pushed her body to the limits. It was an almost spiritual zone. It was as if she were floating above her fatigued body, looking down at her struggle with an inner peace and without the pain normally associated with such exertion. If she could get to this zone when she needed it, she felt confident she could survive this challenge. The training CapHead had devised was pushing her further and further beyond where she was before the World Games. That made sense because the consequence of failure was not disappointment but her own life and likely the lives of her friends and just possibly thirty billion beings as well.

To confirm their beliefs and assumptions, Mona thought she would have a detailed discussion with CapHead. After Mona's last training session for the day, she asked CapHead if they could talk.

CapHead said, "Please, what can I tell you?"

Mona inquired, "The collective is in trouble, is it not?"

CapHead went silent for a moment and said, "The truth is … yes. It has been in trouble for several centuries. The leadership has been corrupted and held on to control only by being brutal, heartless, and paranoid. Our people lack direction, creativity, and any real purpose to live except for self-gratification and a desire to escape boredom. They need not struggle to survive; we only wait for new things to fall into our lap that other civilizations have created and left. Even when we force the amphibians to terra-form the planets left by Chaos, we don't really need the food. We produce enough ourselves within the swarm. We enjoy the new varieties of food; that is all. We just go by the script left by those before us, and we don't know how to change."

Mona said, "Well, Chaos is no more, and you will have to change. The next solar system you visit that contains any competent civilization will easily destroy you. You do know we could have ended your threat at least a year ago?"

CapHead asked, "Why didn't you end us?"

Mona thought and then answered. "I guess we thought better of it. The simple answer is that we almost destroyed ourselves without any help from anyone else. We know the result of unrestricted use of force and destruction and didn't want to destroy thirty billion sentient beings unless we had no other choice. We also wanted to stop the torture and genocide of the amphibian slaves, and we thought their race could possibly help us return our world to its previous life-sustaining condition."

CapHead asked, "What do you want to do now?"

"Well, CapHead," Mona replied, "after this mess with the queen is resolved, you will have a choice. The collective can search the galaxy for a solar system presently devoid of a civilization and colonize it; remain as a self-sustaining collection of ostensibly useless beings, wander forever until you or something more powerful ends you; or perhaps you can use your knowledge, technology, and massive population to help other less-advanced races and civilizations progress. Your choice."

CapHead reflected on his answer and stated, "If I were to lead my people, I would choose a real and better purpose. Their present condition cannot be sustained for much longer. We must rid the collective of the present queen and her form of governance and its corruption in a way that is understood by my people. Mona, I am sure you are the agent of change that can accomplish this miracle. While I have no moral right to ask you, will you go through with the head-to-head competition with Gilda, as is presently scheduled?"

Mona thought to herself, I must be nuts to even consider going through with the competition. We have already obtained the release of Lars2's people. The forces at the swarm's command, while significant, are just sitting ducks for our ships, our technology, and our level of firepower. Unless they can be useful in some way, I am not presently aware of, I just want them to leave. Sue would say that if you hold all the best cards, why draw from the deck looking for anything better? I don't know, except my intuition tells me not to reject his request. Good grief, I don't believe I am going to say … yes. Did I just say … yes?" Mona groaned.

CapHead bowed to Mona and said, "You are more a queen to my race right now than Gilda has been for one hundred years."

"Okay, okay!" Mona groaned again. "I get it; let's not make this too gushy. We need to have our whole planning group jump in on this one. How to change the direction of an entire race?" Mona thought, It would be much easier to kill them all.

The officials were members of the collective's supreme court, who were all selected by the ten tribal leaders and approved by the queen. Gilda had just had her bodyguards personally deliver all the officials a gift basket of body parts from the last state execution. She thought it was such a nice touch, letting them know she was thinking about their professional well-being. Gilda was reviewing the schematics of the weapons Mona had submitted to the competition officials, and while familiar with the bow and arrows, she was totally puzzled by the boomerang. She thought, What a curious knife … She thought the diminutive insect was not going to be much competition and that she might have to make it look closer to improve the drama and make her look better to her public. Oh, what a queen must sacrifice to please her subjects. Now we will just sit and wait. I wonder how a Mona will taste . . . guess it won't be long before I find out.

What is coming next from George and Linda B

From upcoming book: Redemption's Dividends,
Mona Lisa on the Moon Series

A Glimpse of the Future: Chaos got his wish. Mona was not aware of his transformation. The handsome young male humanoid, previously known as the Guardian and before that the diabolically evil Chaos. This new entity was designed and built by Dr. Find and Mona's parents, the schemers kept the miracle of his reanimation their little secret to surprise the object of their affection. So, at the Alliance one-hundred-year Reunion Ball, Chaos Guardian introduced himself to a beautiful woman dressed in a white evening gown, the center of most people's adulation, Captain Mona Ann Lisa. He knelt before her in a warrior costume and asked to dance with her as soon as she got away from the over attentive Emperor Foozle. The good captain festooned in her angel costume was not aware of who Chaos was but was rather charmed by his kneeling and gentle and attentive nature. He said: "Captain Mona Ann Lisa, I would like to thank you for all you have done for the Alliance and especially for me. You are the reason I am here today and experiencing life to the fullest for the first time in an eternity. I am forever in your debt. Please know that I am your friend, and you are my family as are all the Alliance. You were the most capable adversary I ever dueled with in all those eons. You were my better on the battlefield and in so many other ways I cannot explain. You redeemed me from a perpetual hell. I am now and will always be in awe of you and your value as a caring, generous, and beautiful spirit. A true gift to creation." After he said what he had to say he turned and walked away leaving Mona stunned.

About the Authors

Author George B has always been a fan of science fiction, science, religion, fantasy, history, military science, astronomy, theoretical physics, law, medicine, and philosophy. He is now retired but worked for years in several areas of scientific research and application. He started out in the biological sciences, moved to law, was drafted out of law school during the Vietnam War, and later migrated into industrial psychology, computer-assisted analysis, programming, systems analysis, decision analysis, and risk management. Afterward, he transitioned into military science, medicine, artificial intelligence, robotics, and leadership. Throughout, he was known as a troubleshooter and investigator. He was associated with research and development, participating in management and coordination at a national level. He returned to the study of law before finally retiring in 2007. His hobbies include photography, golf, hiking, graphics, research of alternate history, and, of course, writing, not to mention spending time with his dog, Foxy. He shares his life with his very lovely and dear best friend, wife and coauthor of forty-four years, Linda.

My coconspirator, Linda is experienced in the arts and medicine. Linda is a retired teacher, registered nurse, and an accomplished musician. She still teaches piano, and plays the piano (organ occasionally) for our church at services, weddings, and funerals. She is my reality check when it comes to the feminine perspective and rewrites many mistakes and misconceptions. She is a much better wordsmith than I and our combined creative efforts are culminated in this Anthology and many other projects to come.

Go to Amazon and search for Volume 1, Mona Lisa on the Moon, Thirty-Two Thousand Years in the Making

This is the end of our first short story anthology. Linda and I hope you enjoyed a trip into the ancient past and alternate history and mused about the mystical beginnings of humanity. Please join us in the future with adventures from Mona and her crew on the amazing mother ship Dragonfly.